Also by Rosemary Harris

Pushing Up Daisies
The Big Dirt Nap
Dead Head
Slugfest

Short Stories

Growing Up is For Losers
Borrowed Scenery
Do The Math

This is a work of fiction. All of the characters, organizations, locations and events portrayed in this novel are either products of the author's imagination or are used fictitiously.

ISBN 978-0-9896970-1-9
First Edition October 2013

www.rosemaryharris.com

What have readers and reviewers said about Rosemary Harris' books?

"Rosemary Harris is a GEM of a writer!"

—Joanne Fluke, NYTimes best-selling author of the *Hannah Swenson* series

"Smart, sassy and sophisticated, The Bitches of Brooklyn may be the best female buddy book yet."

—Elaine Viets, best-selling author of *Catnapped!* and the *Josie Marcus Mystery Shopper* series.

"...may be a perfect beach read."

—NPR, WSHU's *News Room*

"Fast, funny dialogue, clever description and a good mystery make Harris' latest a very strong, entertaining cozy. With excitement and a surprise ending, this one's a winner. Four stars!"

—*RT Book Reviews*

"a sophisticated mix of comedy, romance and murder could give Harris a wide readership"

—Joe Meyers, *Connecticut Post*

"Quirky, original, and captivating."

—Carolyn Hart, *Agatha, Anthony, and Macavity* award-winning novelist

"Think Diane Mott Davidson's caterer extraordinaire, – Goldy Schulz, or Earlene Fowler's Benni Harper."

—*Omaha World-Herald*

"a sparkling . . . enjoyable series"

—Aunt Agatha's Newsletter Ann Arbor, MI

"An absolute must-read . . . fans of Susan Wittig Albert and Earlene Fowler will relish Harris' exceptionally engaging new voice."

—Julia Spencer Fleming, Edgar finalist and author of *Through the Evil Days*

"a nifty puzzle.."

—*Publishers Weekly*

"Rosemary Harris has quickly become a favorite among mystery fans . . . solid mysteries with great characters, quirky and fun with great plotting. Wonderful dialogue... Harris is a rising star and should be on everyone's bookshelves."

—*Crimespree Magazine*

"A clever mystery...fast-paced and engaging with a heroine who isn't afraid to get down in the dirt."

—*Seattle Post-Intelligencer*

"a funny and entertaining . . . May there be many more."

—*Kingston Observer*

"Hilarious"

—*Kirkus Reviews*

"Pour yourself a glass of wine and get to know Jane Monaghan and her Brooklyn gal pals—the Blackbirds' snarky soul sisters.
Beaches and bonding could be the basis of any group of friends, but betrayal isn't usually part of the package . . . full of smart, hipster fun."

—Nancy Martin, bestselling author of *The Blackbird Sisters Mystery* series

"Laugh out loud funny."

—Harley Jane Kozak, Agatha Award-winning author of *Dating Dead Men*

" . . . with an intriguing mix of . . . sassy wit and smart plotting, Rosemary Harris has crafted a clever mystery."

—Susan Wittig Albert, author of the China Bayles mystery series and *A Wilder Rose*

" . . . place, character and sprightly dialogue. And the scene in which the villain is unmasked is highly original."

—Joanne Collings, *Bookpage*

"a blooming good mystery debut . . . introduces a gutsy heroine with an offbeat supporting cast."

—Lesa Holstine, librarian, *Lesa's Book Critiques*

"an exciting, well-plotted amateur sleuth due to a quirky heroine and an eccentric supporting cast."

—Harriet Klausner, *Genre Go Round Reviews*

About the Author

Rosemary Harris is a native Brooklynite, born in Fort Greene and raised in Flatbush like some of the characters in *The Bitches of Brooklyn*. Her debut novel in the Dirty Business Mystery series, the Agatha and Anthony-nominated, *Pushing Up Daisies*, was followed by *The Big Dirt Nap, Dead Head* and *Slugfest.*

She is past president of Mystery Writers of America's NY Chapter and Sisters in Crime's New England Chapter and is a member of Romance Writers of America, and Connecticut Authors and Publishers Association. She lives in New York City and Fairfield County, CT.

Visit Rosemary at **www.rosemaryharris.com** and Like her on facebook at **www.facebook.com/RosemaryHarriswriter**

The Bitches of Brooklyn

ROSEMARY HARRIS

CHESTNUT HILL BOOKS
NEW YORK • CONNECTICUT

“Whenever anyone has called me a bitch,
I have taken it as a compliment.”

—*Margaret Cho*

CHAPTER 1

As deliveries went, this one was somewhere between a balloon telegram and a bulletproof vest wrapped around a dead fish. Most gift baskets arrived with cards bearing congratulations or condolences. Rarely were they sent with the simple two-line message Jane Monaghan stared at, then read, in disbelief, a second time.

A skinny delivery boy hovered in the doorway, shifting his weight and waiting for a tip. Jane fumbled in her handbag, she never had singles when she needed them. As she poked through her voluminous bag, the boy peered inside the house, curious about the women renting the old Beninger place. He remembered the first year they came. His mother had warned him to keep his distance and his father had slipped him a sly wink he'd been too young to interpret.

They were neither young nor old, that gray area between youth and invisibility. Still good for a nooner, the boy fantasized, using an expression he'd learned from his Uncle Billy. If he could cut one from the herd. Not the one who'd answered the door – she was out of his league.

Maybe the small, dark-haired one sprawled on the loveseat near the fireplace. She had a nubby throw tossed over one leg but the other was exposed in all its glory – tan, taut and barely covered by denim short shorts. Still pretty hot, even if she looked old enough to have been his – what . . . babysitter? Who hadn't had that fantasy?

The hot one and the boy made eye contact. Having been on the receiving end of similar looks for close to twenty years – longer than *he'd* been alive – it took Tina Ruggiero all of thirty seconds to read his mind.

"Come back in a few years, sonny. Let's wait until that acne clears up."

The boy's naughty daydream evaporated. His face reddened and he regressed to bumbling, pimply errand boy. His eyes grew watery. He even looked shorter, if that was possible. Jane abandoned her search for singles, shoved a five in his direction and kicked the storm door shut.

"A day without a verbal castration is like a day without sunshine?"

"Come on," Tina said. "He asked for it – gawking like that. Half the people in this town think we're practicing witchcraft and the other half think we're gay. Not that I don't think you're all cute. I just wanted to set the record straight."

Jane wasn't sure the exchange wouldn't have the opposite effect, convincing him she *was* a witch, only he'd spell it with a "b." That was fitting since it was what they'd been dubbed a long time ago when they were teens, The Bitches of Brooklyn. Were they really? Depended on who you asked.

"A new wrinkle has been added to our weekend," Jane said, looking at the card that came with the basket.

"Not another one. I already have a new wrinkle, that's why I cut bangs."

"I wondered what that was about. I thought it might

have been advice from our missing friend."

Jane carried the oversized basket to the wooden dining table, where Clare Didrikson and Rachel Weiner, two of her closest friends, sat with their morning coffees.

The table and chairs were like all the furniture in the rented house – ancient wood or wicker upon which thousands of summer memories had been made, or brand new, from the discount store, because who would buy good furniture for a house through which total strangers traipsed three months every year? Jane pulled out a chair and read the card aloud to the group.

"It's a joke," Tina said. She flung off the blanket and hopped over on her one good leg to join them and see for herself. "Just like her to bail at the last minute and then pull a stunt like this. She's probably laughing her ass off somewhere, ordering the *next* fruit basket with the *next* cryptic message. *Luca Brasi sleeps with the fishes! Go to the hayfield, there'll be a volcanic rock that has no earthly business in a Maine hayfield.* She's always so melodramatic. Can't she just admit something better came up?"

It was not the first time their absent friend had cancelled at the last minute even though the dates were fixed well in advance. The other four understood, but there was a trace of resentment, too. As if it was a given the fifth woman's time was more valuable than theirs.

The four women settled around the table in the weather-beaten Cape Cod bungalow they rented every summer for the last six years. They met for the same late August weekend when husbands and partners were otherwise engaged, either of their own accord or dispatched so the women wouldn't feel guilty about leaving four men, one daughter, one veterinary practice, and two businesses for much girl talk and more alcohol in an ocean beach setting far removed from their Brooklyn beginnings.

Initially, they played "remember when" and speculated on what had happened to friends from the old neighborhood. That first year Rachel brought her laptop and their old high school yearbook, and between drinks and steamers they Googled and giggled over former boyfriends and teachers, most of whom had lost their hair, gotten heavy, or somehow morphed into mere mortals instead of the brooding geniuses and bohemian heartthrobs they'd once seemed. After that it was agreed – no laptops at The Weekend.

Clare reached for the card, looking for what? Some explanation hidden between the lines? Some tone or nuance conveyed in the elegant script of an anonymous clerk in a New England gift shop? She chewed on her lower lip but said nothing.

Jane tugged on the purple ribbon at the top of the basket, untying the bow and releasing the twisted cellophane. She wound the ribbon around four fingers as if saving it for some future use, which wasn't likely since they'd all be home in a few days. Back to real life. Unless what was written in the note was true and real life would be forever changed. A hidden staple pierced one slim, unmanicured finger and she sucked on it while poking through the basket with her undamaged hand.

"At least she sprang for the good stuff." Jane held up a red foil-covered brick. "Real cheese, not cheese product."

"And candy," Rachel said. "Just what we need."

Tina and Jane plundered the basket, Jane moving through the items and inspecting ingredients. "Cream crackers, no partially hydrogenated anything so far." Jane was co-owner of a small bakery called Sweet Dreams and paid attention to such things. Tina wasn't so picky. Two grunts and an arched eyebrow told her the others were less appreciative of their missing friend's nutritional considerations.

"Belgian chocolates. Scottish cookies," Jane said, still sucking on her punctured finger.

"Please don't get blood on anything," Tina said. "If there are shortbread cookies, I've got dibs. I don't care if they have lard in them but I draw the line at bodily fluids."

Despite Rachel's protestations, the chocolate would disappear first. Even the boring sucking candies would go, and all that would remain was a tasteful brown basket, some purple ribbon and the note –

Apologies for the short notice
but I won't be making our little reunion this year.
I've run off with one of your men.

—Abby

CHAPTER 2

Tina half-stood in her seat, readjusted her ankle and groaned as she reached across the table. "Let me see that card."

There was silence, then nervous laughter, as Tina delivered the lines again and again, each time with an even more theatrical flourish, all she'd retained from two years of acting classes discontinued when she realized she not only would never be Meryl Streep, she wouldn't even be Susan Lucci.

"It's probably my dentist," Tina said. "The girl is *messing* with us."

The f–bomb came more naturally to Tina and ordinarily she would have dropped it, instead of the gentler "messing" but it would have betrayed an anger she didn't really feel. And her salty language sometimes ruffled Clare who'd grown more conservative since moving to Connecticut. Tina tossed the card on the table and sat down again, resting her left ankle on one of the unused chairs.

"It's her warped idea of a joke. She'll come waltzing in with half a dozen lobsters and a twenty-two year old lobsterman who's packing a sea monster. Probably the delivery boy's older, blemish-free cousin. Then she'll dismiss him and tell us how they nearly capsized his boat when he whipped out Nessie."

Or they'd learn the following week that Abby Daniels had flown to the West Coast having added a budding rap star to her client roster. Or to Europe to meet with the chairman of a new line of luxury goods. Hadn't they all lived vicariously through her exploits – even when she was a teen? The travel, the non-traditional home life? The glamorous parents? Although anyone else's parents were more glamorous than one's own.

But around the table, clutching cups of now-cold coffee a pair of faces had darkened. Maybe Abby's note was a joke but two of the women took it seriously. History had taught them the fifth woman was capable of a great many things. Particularly when it came to men.

Of the four, Rachel Weiner, Clare Didrikson (then Gibson), and Tina Ruggiero had known each other since third grade. They were from Brooklyn, New York – *before* Brooklyn became hipster haven, the obligatory pit stop for every young person on the planet wanting to be an artist or work in publishing. When Brooklyn was still known as the home of Walt Whitman and Norman Mailer and not just the place where Heath Ledger and Jay-Z once lived.

They had grown up in a neighborhood of smallish apartment buildings and modest homes just beginning to bounce back from two decades of economic depression. Their parents had reversed the exodus of the previous generation and moved downtown from Midwood, Sheepshead Bay and Flatbush in search of smart real estate deals. And they'd found them. Tina's family on the lower end of the financial spectrum, Clare's on the higher and Rachel's somewhere in between, although none of the families was rich.

The girls had been so close it wasn't unusual for friends and even teachers to run all their names together and refer to them as RachelClaranTina as if they were one exotic person. *RachelClaranTina!* The click of castanets or the stomp of flamenco heels should have followed.

Sandy-haired and athletic, with a former swimmer's shoulders, Rachel was always first to raise her hand, to volunteer them for some activity. To suggest they raise money for the animal shelter or put on a play at the local senior center. Her mother, Gilda, was obsessed with college applications and had driven home early the value of extra-curricular activities.

Tina was the smart-ass, her long, dark hair and strong features she'd never quite grow into contributing to her sultry look and convincing men and boys – like the hapless delivery kid – that she'd be a wild woman in bed if only they could make it happen. With three older brothers she learned to handle male attention at an early age and could deflate a man as quickly as she could do the opposite.

Clare was the glue. She still was. A smart, pretty blonde with what the other parents referred to as *a good head on her shoulders*, Clare had been their Get-Out-of-Jail-Free card. When they were kids she kept them out of serious trouble because her wholesome look and responsible nature convinced authority figures that the trio couldn't possibly be responsible for whatever mischief had occurred. Even if they were guilty as sin.

Jane Monaghan's family moved to the area later, when the girls entered eighth grade. Not a great time to be uprooted and thrust into a new school where her classmates all seemed to have known each other since they were in utero.

Another girl might have had a harder time of it, but

Jane had two things going for her. One, she was lovely in that quiet child-woman way that hinted at the knockout she'd become in a few short years. And two, Jane's stay-at-home mom was a world-class baker who sent her to school every day with cupcakes and cookies that were minor works of art – unusual shapes, fanciful icing patterns and decorations that, fueled by alcohol and some said drugs, she worked on well into the night so they'd be fresh for Jane's lunchbox the next morning. Perhaps that was the mother's strategy to ease her daughter's transition – and her own – to the new environment.

"Is it too early for wine?" Tina could always break the tension.

It *was* too early. But they were on vacation. And it wasn't scandalously early like the time Clare's book club friend entered a meeting at nine a.m. on a Monday morning, strode to Clare's credenza and poured herself a stiff one before announcing that she was leaving the book group, and by the way, her husband was leaving her. They never did discuss *The History of Love*, it didn't seem appropriate. Or maybe they did discuss it and just didn't realize it.

"Stay there," Rachel said, "I'll get the wine." Tina had been hopping all over the house since they arrived because of a bicycle collision she'd had near Grand Army Plaza. It was only a matter of time before she would injure the other ankle.

Rachel unfolded herself from the chair closest to the kitchen area and retrieved one of the bottles they'd brought to the Cape. Every year they packed a case of good wine along with a hamper of healthy treats unlikely to be found at the general store. This let the women perpetuate the myth they were "being good" even though by the middle of the weekend they'd be at the drive-in chowing down on tubs of popcorn and salty, chemical-laden snacks as if they were still teenagers. This year, thanks to Abby, hunks of cheese and Belgian chocolates would hasten their downward spiral.

They'd all struggled with weight issues. What teenage girl doesn't think she's either too fat or too thin? A perfectionist, Clare had had a brush with bulimia. Jane didn't agonize about her weight but she was mindful of it living in an apartment filled with more chocolate chips and sprinkles than wholesome food – her mother's skill in the kitchen didn't extend to mundane dishes like chicken or fish.

With Rachel, the obsession was a holdover from the days she needed to get her weight down for swim meets. Parading before hundreds of people in an unflattering tank suit was one of the traumas of her adolescence and she still bore the scars. Over The Bitches annual weekend she unconsciously announced the calorie count of every item purchased or consumed until the others pleaded with her to stop. Only Tina was naturally slim and she joked that was because her brothers ate all the good stuff.

Rachel rummaged through one utensil drawer after another looking for a corkscrew. She must have wanted a drink badly because the longer it took, the more noise she made, and the louder the drawer slams. Except for Jane, the women always drank more when they were together. Maybe it was to feel young again without the realities of mortgage payments, children, aging parents, fledgling businesses and maturing relationships.

"Is that the same kind of wine we had last night?" Jane asked, after the third drawer slammed shut.

"Why? Do we need a special wine pairing to go with

cream crackers and bad news?"

Jane joined her friend at the counter and quietly unscrewed the cap from the wine bottle.

"I'm a bitch."

"Yes, you are."

That was a familiar exchange ever since they'd been in high school. The first line covered all manner of transgressions from not responding to an email fast enough to wearing the same color to a party. It had started as an insult flung by a jealous classmate. A nod to a popular book and movie, *The Witches of Eastwick*. But the girls had co-opted it, changing the appellation from an insult to, if not a compliment, at least a frisky nickname for the group that none of them had really minded.

"Sit," Jane said. "As the resident foodie, I'll do the honors."

She wiped the already clean wine glasses with a threadbare dish towel that had been hanging on an old-fashioned pegboard near the stove. She held each glass up to the light, inspecting for spots and lint. Then she set them on the counter, filling three and pouring herself a club soda with just a splash of the wine. Jane had a predisposition for alcohol that was a legacy from her mother along with hazel eyes, fair skin and an affinity for baking. She was a little too susceptible to the stuff and knew to be cautious.

The women drank up and Jane topped them off. One bottle down. They were edgier than any of them cared to admit. No one wanted to believe what the note implied. And who wanted to be first to reach for her phone to see if her husband was on his way to an assignation with one of their closest friends?

Not that their phones would have worked. On that part of the Cape, locals joked that the wind had to blow in a certain direction and the planets had to be in alignment for cell service to work and even then you had to stand on the dune, which was neither smart, safe, nor allowed because the dunes were eroding, slipping into the sea at an alarming and dangerous rate.

The year-rounders had seen to this enforced solitude much to the consternation of the summer renters, who claimed to enjoy the feeling of detachment and seclusion but were secretly irritated when they couldn't be connected at will. The visitors could be seen, early in the morning, sitting in their cars pretending not to be checking emails in the parking lot outside the general store where the cell signal was strong.

We can be online and always accessible when we're home, Clare had said. We don't need anyone else here, we have each other.

And they had. They'd been a self-contained unit since high school when they met the fifth woman, Abby Daniels.

CHAPTER 3

She was neither the prettiest of the five (that was Jane) nor the smartest (Clare) but everyone agreed Abby Daniels had something that set her apart. She could take your breath away with a smile or freeze you out by its absence. When she paid you the slightest attention it was as if the sun had come out from behind the clouds. There was something in the way she carried herself, her posture, her manner of speaking – not peppered with the giggles and "you knows" of other girls her age. And Abby and her father had purchased a large corner brownstone and practically singlehandedly jumpstarted the neighborhood's gentrification. People were almost grateful to be around Abby and MacGregor Daniels.

They had lived up and down the East Coast and abroad by the time Abby was thirteen, moving each time the foundation Mac worked for sent him to vet another worthy cause. By the time they'd relocated to Brooklyn, Abby had a smattering of French and Spanish and was fluent in Italian having spent two years in Rome where her father was immersed in a project that funded the restoration of major works of art. Her mother was also immersed in things Italian. The year Abby turned fourteen, his name was Paolo and when her husband's project ended, Maria Daniels chose to remain in Italy with him instead of returning to the States.

At her new school, Abby's teachers took an instant shine to her. She made them feel brilliant and worldly by feeding them back their own lines and casually dropping references to places she and her father had visited – Havana, Berlin, Nairobi. From someone else it might have sounded obnoxious, but not from Abby. She wasn't bragging. It was simply her resume.

Even the notoriously un-charmable algebra teacher Miss Friedland was won over after Abby noticed and admired a pendant the teacher had worn – a souvenir from a much-loved and oft-mentioned trip to Mexico where the other students had unkindly speculated that Miss Friedland had known her one and only sexual experience, probably involving an exchange of pesos.

There just wasn't anyone who didn't believe Abby Daniels was wonderful. This should have made the other girls loathe her, but Abby's greatest talent was in making *you* believe she thought *you* were the most interesting person in the room. That was irresistible. She could charm the pants off anyone. And frequently did.

None of the women could explain how they had drifted apart after high school. First college, then husbands, new locations and new interests reduced their friendships to emails and scribbled missives inserted into holiday cards. *We went to London. I sold a story. Kate made the swim team.* Clare sent family newsletters heralding every minor television production her husband Brian worked on, updates on her fertility issues and later the Ukrainian baby she hoped to adopt.

Nothing bad had happened, it was just life. As close as they'd once been time, distance and inevitability conspired to keep them apart – until the year a fellow classmate organized an informal reunion.

When the Bitches were teens every Friday night was spent at a local hangout. During the week the location was a non-descript intersection – a deli, a church, a movie theatre and a convenience store. A landmark high school that some old-time Hollywood stars had attended stood nearby. But on Friday nights the corner turned into a mecca for every high school student in the borough. Kids from public schools and private. Catholic schools or yeshivas. More crowded than any school play, dance or football game, the corner belonged to teenagers – sharing secrets, cigarettes and first kisses. Hearts were broken, dreams were shared and lifelong friendships and enmities were forged. Rachel, Clare, Tina, Jane and Abby had held court on the southwest corner near the old-fashioned ice cream parlor where claiming it was your birthday could score you a free banana split.

It was a surprise then, when almost fifteen years later, the five women found themselves in a midtown Manhattan restaurant. At the reunion.

They ignored the hundred or so other attendees – grown men working hard to regain their boyish swagger, women faring a little better with only a few squished into too tight or too youthful clothing. The Bitches camped out in a dark corner of the bar long after everyone else had exhausted their mild curiosity and temporary joy at seeing one another.

"Here's to the Bitches," they'd laughed. "All present and accounted for!"

After the reunion, they slipped into an easy routine of

emails, occasional dinners and day trips to the Hamptons or the Jersey Shore which, given their varied lifestyles and locations, took weeks to coordinate, especially for Rachel who now lived near Pittsburgh, the equivalent of Ulan Battar to a Brooklynite. She was also the only one with a child, ten-year-old Kate.

When someone in Clare's office told her about a house rental on Cape Cod, it sounded perfect for an all-girls getaway. A four bedroom bungalow at the end of a road off Ocean Drive, perched on the edge of a dune, one steep staircase to the beach. The usual renters had needed to cancel unexpectedly and a last-minute rental was possible if they could commit that day.

Spending an entire weekend together would be risky. It would force their relationships into the present. Perhaps old friends were best kept in the past, that way you didn't risk damaging fond memories. They would never lose their places in your heart or reveal themselves to be obvious or pretentious. Or worse still – stupid.

Nevertheless, the availability of the house was serendipitous and the fact that everyone's schedule had meshed – even Abby's, who always said she'd *try* to make dinner or lunch without making a firm commitment until the last minute – was looked upon as a sign. So they took the rental and became the new regulars for that week.

Sometimes Rachel left western Pennsylvania early to visit her mother in Brooklyn. Tina and Jane, who still lived there, joined her for the drive to Connecticut and they'd pile into Clare's SUV for the longer part of the journey. They would drive north, listening to oldies, stopping at outlet stores and sampling lobster rolls and fried clams all the way up the coast.

Abby always arrived by herself. This time she'd try to

meet them at Clare's but if her last meeting went long they should go on without her. She'd either take the train to Boston and the ferry to Provincetown where they could pick her up, or she'd fly to Hyannis and get to Wellfleet on her own. Either way, Abby said she would be in touch.

They just didn't think it would be via fruit basket.

Tina took a deep swig of Vouvray as if it was lemonade on a scorching hot day.

"Slow down, cowgirl. It may be cocktail hour in another time zone but it's only about 11 a.m. here in Massachusetts."

"This is strictly for medicinal purposes, Clare. I forgot to pack the resveratrol."

"I think it's only red wine that has resveratrol," Rachel said.

"Thank you, Dr. Weiner. Don't worry," Tina said, "I'm not going on a bender. Truth be told – Abby can *have* my husband," She spoke in a cavalier tone the others weren't completely buying. "We haven't even hit the two-year mark. I still have old boyfriends I dated longer than I've been with David. Hell, I have *nail polish* I've had longer. Besides, do you have any idea how impossible it is to have two struggling writers in one family?"

They did. She talked about it so often they could probably repeat it back to her verbatim.

Tina was a soon-to-be-published novelist, teaching in a private school in lower Manhattan. Her mother had drummed into her head the idea of becoming a teacher because to Mama Ruggiero's generation, teaching and nursing were nice safe jobs where women, like the good Italian girls Tina's older brothers had chosen, could "do something useful" before they settled down and got married. Feminism had not yet reached the Ruggiero household.

A fledgling acting career, which had consisted of one

walk-on for a soap and one line that she flubbed, was mercifully before the advent of TiVo so not many of her friends were witnesses. Eventually, without a Plan B and much to her mother's delight – Tina abandoned her dreams of becoming the next Oscar winner from Brooklyn and found herself grudgingly applying for her teacher's license.

Surprisingly she didn't hate teaching – just most of the parents, pampered little shits who assumed that a smile and the occasional gift card from Bliss or Sephora would nudge their kid's grades higher. Sad to say, the tactic worked with some of her colleagues and at times Tina found herself wondering why in the world she was paying for her own moisturizer when so many desperate parents were willing to do it for her.

For a laugh she started scribbling down some of the more ridiculous incidents at the school and strung them into a loose narrative which she posted anonymously on a neighborhood blog. When a literary agent tracked her down and promised Tina a book deal, she had visions of flinging her locker key on the principal's desk and walking out to a waiting stretch limo. But her advance was so small it would barely cover the cost of a new dress and the party she'd be expected to throw herself to launch the book.

Tina's husband David was also a writer. A slash person actually. Currently he was a poet/novelist/freelancer/editor who worked at one of the publishing houses which didn't buy the rights to Tina's book. They'd met at a one-day writer's event which had been pitched as speed-dating with a publishing executive. In their case, the description had been accurate.

There had been an immediate attraction and much mutual eye-rolling as the wannabee writer on line in front of Tina delivered a stream-of-consciousness pitch about the motivations of Lothar, her sex-crazed alien protagonist. Tina and David referenced Lothar whenever they stood in a long queue, one of many small jokes that constituted a private shorthand between them.

As a group The Bitches had attended two or three of David's open microphone readings in the East Village. Most recently they'd gathered in a dimly lit basement club where David recited disjointed verse which left most listeners confused except for the other performers who stood and applauded furiously, anxious to move him off the stage so they could torture their own friends and family.

Abby had pronounced his recitation "brave" and she presented him with a slim anthology that included works by a poet they'd discussed at length at a dinner party months before and the gift won Abby a permanent place of honor in David's heart. He was flattered. He sought her approval more than any of the others, including his wife since Tina *had* to say she loved his performance, even if she didn't. Tina was touched that her old friend had been kind to her husband but, that volume of poetry was the first thing she thought of when Abby's note arrived.

Was it David?

"Do you remember that night?" Tina said. "They went gaga over some dead Peruvian."

"Brazilian," Clare said. "And I'm fairly sure he's still alive."

"Jeez, Clare – whatever. I'm making a point. For all I know, they might be feeding each other grapes and reading excruciating, self-indulgent verse to each other right now. Not that I would be crushed." Once again she did her best to seem unconcerned.

"Not a chance. David has no money." Jane was sorry the instant she blurted it out. Alcohol-wise, she was a lightweight. It was in the genes. Even a splash of wine dissolved the filter that normally kept people from saying the first inappropriate thing that popped into their heads.

"Bitch," Tina said, with a smile. "Easy for you. You've got one regular and one spare."

The "one regular" was Jane's live-in boyfriend, Vincenzo Palmieri, who worked with her at Sweet Dreams. The "one spare" was a reference to Jane's business partner, Glenn Buonofiglio, a flirty, macho guy, the son of the bakery's former owner.

Tina raised her glass. "Here's to all the Bitches, absent and present." It was a variation of their familiar toast and that day it took on a different meaning.

A show of hands would have revealed that Rachel, Tina, Clare and Jane *all* thought Abby a little too fond of the good life to run away with an underpaid editor who made money on the side writing blurbs for an online shopping site. True, it required talent to get consumers excited over a twelve-inch frittata pan with a non-stick surface, but it wasn't exactly the stuff that dreams were made of, particularly, if like Abby, you were used to exchanging small talk with heads of companies and the occasional celebrity.

Rachel's husband wasn't a likely candidate either and she'd be the first to say so. Rachel was a veterinarian with a thriving suburban practice near Oakmont and she was thought by the group to be the breadwinner in her family. Her husband had a state job with some nebulous connection to organic farming. Even Rachel found it difficult to keep her eyelids from drooping when Bob Price discussed his work. And he was co-founder of the local food co-op which Rachel supported in principle but found deadly dull, filled with too earnest women in baggy clothes and Birkenstocks. She just wanted fresh produce and wanted to be able to pick up a copy of *People* or *InStyle* when she went to the market to get some without feeling guilty or shallow.

Bob grew organic tomatoes, in upside down hanging planters – as seen on television – which fringed the porch of their Pennsylvania home. He could bloviate on the subject of heirloom tomatoes until your eyes glazed over and you silently vowed to never eat pizza or marinara sauce again. Not-so-secretly The Bitches referred to him as Tomato Bob.

The odds of Abby running off with Tomato Bob were about equal to the odds of George Clooney ringing their doorbell and asking to borrow a cup of sugar. Buck naked.

Jane's boyfriend was another story. Vincenzo Palmieri was drop-dead gorgeous. He was five years younger than she. Italian. From Italy. With those qualities he could have been an organ grinder or a professional balloon artist and women would still have wanted to run away with him. That he could cook was an enormous plus. Even the way he said *gnocchi* was sexy. Jane had met him five years earlier at a party.

Abby Daniels introduced them.

CHAPTER 4

"Abby is not going to ruin our weekend. I refuse to sit here and get loaded in the afternoon just because she got a better offer," Rachel said. "Maybe we can't go bike riding because of Tina's ankle, but there are plenty of other activities. We can visit galleries in Provincetown or go whale watching."

"Go without me," Tina said. "Please. I *can* get loaded in the afternoon. I have extensive experience. I brought a stack of magazines and my work-in-progress, and all the basic food groups I'm interested in are represented in that damn basket. I won't starve – either intellectually or physically."

"Nope," Jane said. "Rachel's right. This is The Weekend and we're on the Cape. We're supposed to eat fried food and things with cranberries in them and buy prints we'll never have framed and will leave in the closet."

"Yes," Rachel added, "preferably in establishments decorated with fishing nets and buoys. C'mon, these people rely on the tourist trade and we haven't contributed our fair share to the local economy this season. It's our civic duty."

They stood, arms folded, waiting for Tina to be won over.

"Are you two from the Chamber of Commerce? Clare, help me out here." Tina pleaded, but Clare's facial expression said she was on their side.

"If Abby was here," Tina said, "she'd respect my decision."

"We respect your decision," Rachel said, "we just want you to change it."

Tina pondered the logic of that statement, but not for long. "All right," Tina said, "*No mas*. I can't take on all of you. It would be a tragedy if we came back next year and the muffin store had changed hands because we didn't spend enough money this week."

"That's the spirit."

Clare made the plan. "Your ankle may be out of commission but there's nothing wrong with your arms. Instead of bikes we can rent two tandem kayaks at Pedal and Paddle," she said. "We'll have a picnic at one of the ponds. Don't worry you can bring the wine – I'll be the designated driver."

She gave them each assignments and the three able-bodied women packed a lunch and trekked back and forth to the car loading food, towels, blankets and gear into Clare's SUV while Tina sat in a folding beach chair and critiqued. Periodically she'd cross and recross her legs, wincing theatrically.

"You're getting a lot of mileage out of that Ace bandage. It's a cheap ploy to get sympathy, isn't it?" Jane said. "How exactly did you earn that merit badge? One of the mean girls at school give you a swift kick?"

Tina shook her head. "Bicycle mishap near Prospect Park. This crazy broad in a Mercedes sideswiped me. I swear she was aiming for me. I swerved to avoid her and got too close to a line of parked cars. My foot got caught in the spokes. Took me a while to stop so my ankle got a little chewed up. Not broken, but sprained and bloody."

"Ouch," Jane said. "You're officially excused from manual labor. You couldn't have made that up."

"Yes, I could, I'm a writer, I lie for a living, remember? Well, it's not a living yet. A couple of neighborhood kids thought it was hysterical. Two years ago, I would have knocked the little pishers down and pretended it was unavoidable, but I found myself thinking – *just kill them off in the next book.*"

"A true humanitarian," Clare said. "Remind me not to let you babysit for me."

"Would this be a bad time to remind you that you *have* no children?"

"Yes, Bitch. Now take a seat before we vote to strap you to the roof of the car."

Once the gear was assembled, they collected personal items – a change of clothing, hats, and sweaters in case the Cape weather took a turn for the worse.

Jane was impressed by Clare's packing strategy. "Do you ever put this much stuff in your car when we're not with you?" Jane asked.

"Spoken like a city girl. Of course, we do. Ask Rachel. She lives in the suburbs. And she's got a kid. Once the baby is here, as big as this car is, it will probably be too small. The house may even be too small. You wouldn't think an infant could require so much gear but I've been doing my homework. There won't be a room in the house without her stamp on it."

Jane thought it sounded horrid but wisely kept it to herself. Whether it was her own Spartan upbringing or Vincenzo's tales of his simple childhood in Treviso, she was convinced that when she had children, they would not need so many material things. And when they did she would purchase them in tasteful, non-primary colors, then recycle the items to other like-minded parents. But then . . . what did she know?

Clare shifted the cooler in the back of the car so there was no chance of it tipping over. "With this vehicle," she said, admiring her handiwork, "we engage in the suburban equivalent of hunting and gathering. We go out empty every weekend and come back with food, tag sale treasures, plants, tools." She touched and fine-tuned everything the others had put in the car, confirming Jane's unspoken belief that no two people ever packed a suitcase, a car or a dishwasher in quite the same way.

"How's the adoption going?" Tina asked. "When does the bundle of joy arrive?"

Maybe one of the worst things you could ask a woman waiting for a baby adoption to come through.

Clare had smiled through the first four years of her marriage to Brian as thoughtless relatives asked over and over again about the absence of a baby bump. She'd grown to hate that term. A bump. Like it was a pimple or a fibroid. The result of too many beers at happy hour. Whatever it was, Clare and Brian had not been able to produce a bump although it was not for want of trying. At least early in their marriage.

"She's not a FedEx delivery. Brian and I fly to Kiev next month and stay for three weeks. We might have gotten her sooner but his schedule is packed and both adopting parents have to be there to pick up the baby. The authorities at the child welfare agency are very strict about that. Single parent adoptions aren't permitted and people have tried to game the system by pretending to be married."

The others nodded knowingly, but as the sole mother in the group, only Rachel knew what Clare was letting herself in for. She'd help, if asked, but Clare had wanted a child for so long, she had ten years' worth of how-to books, DVDs and parenting advice stacked up and ready to be unleashed on the poor unsuspecting orphan. Some of it was probably already outdated.

They took off for Pedal and Paddle, located in the same strip as the general store, a small post office and a liquor store. Clare pulled into a spot closest to the rental shop so they wouldn't have far to carry the kayaks.

Someone suggested cold drinks and everyone agreed. Rachel claimed she needed sunscreen. Jane was suddenly compelled to send a postcard to her employees at Sweet Dreams – "otherwise she'd get home before the card did." Tina stayed in the backseat of the car with her injured limb propped on a stack of beach towels piled on the divider between the two front seats. With the others gone she amused herself by sliding down and attempting to turn up the volume on the radio with her big toe.

After fifteen minutes, a pair of deeply-tanned, golden-haired boys in open shirts, flowered swim trunks and flip-flops brought out two fiberglass kayaks and hoisted them hull side up onto the rack on top of Clare's car.

"Good lord," Tina muttered.

The boys wedged foam blocks in between the boats and yanked hard on nylon tie-down straps so the kayaks wouldn't rattle or shift in transit. From inside, Tina ate up the view of rippling twenty-year-old abs and shorts hanging deliciously low on the wearers' hips. Good grief, she thought, if David has run off with Abby, I'm staying here. God bless phone cameras. She pulled out her phone and snapped a few headless torso shots.

By the time her friends returned the boats had been secured and paddles, seats and life jackets stowed. Tina passed around her phone so the others could admire the youthful bodies they'd missed seeing.

"Very nice," Jane said.

Seated up front Rachel agreed and held the phone to let Clare see but she shook her head, eyes half-closed. "You're gonna like the way they look," Rachel said. "I guarantee it."

"Not interested."

"Look who's so highly evolved she can't enjoy a little beefcake," Tina said. "I should accidentally on purpose send these pictures to David, in case he's getting any ideas. Let him stew for a while."

She wouldn't really send them and he wouldn't really stew. They were the newlyweds in the group and the assumption was that Tina and David still had romantic dinners, called each other pet names and made love in every room in their apartment – possibly even in the small, old-fashioned elevator in their pre-war building. But then, that might have been wishful thinking.

The pond was only three miles away but Clare took it slow. Always a cautious driver, she seemed more so that day with the kayaks strapped to the car. You never knew when something you thought was secure could suddenly become unmoored, even though Tina had asked the boys to use extra tie-downs and bungee cords (so she could take more pictures.) All the women were strangely silent. Hands fixed at ten-ten on the steering wheel, Clare spoke first.

"All right, I'll put you out of your misery. I checked voicemail while I was in the rental shop. It's Brian she's run off with. We've been having problems."

Clare's husband had left a message that there had been sudden interest from the BBC in his documentary and he'd flown to London for a meeting. He didn't say when he'd be back. Clare had always been supportive of Brian, and so had her parents who'd lent him seed money for the project. But she had a hard time believing the home of *I, Claudius* and *Upstairs, Downstairs* would be considering Brian's exhaustive and exhausting look at the history of comic books.

"He's too busy to go to Kiev to pick up our daughter but for The Justice League of America he can drop everything."

"It could be his big break." Rachel tried to sound as if she meant it. She liked Brian but thought he suffered from a case of arrested development. Grown men who collected action figures always made her queasy.

Clare kept quiet. She sat at the intersection longer than necessary, her classic features without expression, like a finely chiseled death mask. Then Jane broke the silence.

"Vincenzo's gone to Italy. I talked to my assistant manager. He said there was a family emergency with one of his brothers and had to leave. He doesn't even *like* that brother," she added, almost to herself.

Tina started laughing.

"And this is funny because. . . . ?" Jane asked.

"I'm sorry. It *is* funny. I didn't mean to, but I had my phone out to capture the surfer dudes and afterward I instinctively checked emails. It was totally unconscious. One of the writers scheduled to teach a two-week course in Tuscany was diagnosed with shingles and had to cancel. My husband is on his way to Italy, too. Maybe they're meeting for a threesome."

Jane turned to Rachel to see if her sudden need for SPF40 had been an excuse to check on her own husband. But Tomato Bob was virtually unreachable, camping on the White Rim Road in Utah, and unless Rachel wanted to pay $40,000 for the National Park Service to do an aerial search she'd simply have to sit tight until he got in touch.

"Look," Rachel said, "we encourage them to go away while we're here, don't we?"

That was true enough. Once they'd even suggested their men vacation together but that was vetoed after one all-guys drinks-and-pizza date that went south fast after Tomato Bob insisted on bringing his own home-made wine to the restaurant.

Behind them, a driver leaned on his horn.

"Not me, sister, I'm working. Take a freakin' vote and decide which way to turn. Four women in a car and not one of them can drive." He shook his head in disgust.

Uncharacteristically, Clare uttered a four-letter word and made an anatomically impossible suggestion none of the others had ever heard her make before.

Tina let out a low whistle and patted her friend on the shoulder. "Beneath the velvet headband vestiges of the Brooklyn Bitch remain. I'm proud of you."

As the loutish driver suggested, they did take a vote and on the count of three all four women stuck their arms out of the windows and shot the man the bird before making a hard, screeching left. If Tina had been at full-strength, she would have mooned him.

CHAPTER 5

"Damn, that was like the old days," Tina said, settling back into her seat as they drove off. "Why don't we do more stuff like that?"

"Uh – because we're grown-ups?" Jane said.

"Speak for yourself. Is that it now? We're geezers? Didn't it feel good letting that Neanderthal know what we thought of him?"

"I can't afford to let anyone know what I really think of them. They may be potential customers," Jane said. "You'll learn that once your book comes out. In fact I don't even really like you guys, I just want to sell you cupcakes."

"Funny."

"I'll admit it," Rachel said. "Briefly, it felt good. But that trucker – instead of being your garden variety misogynist who assumes women can't operate heavy machinery – could have been a road rage psycho. One of those lunatics who runs you off the road, drugs you and then takes you to an underground dungeon somewhere."

"Au contraire. If anything we should have an Ashley Judd film festival next year." Rachel said. "Did you see the one where her husband frames her for his own death and then puts her in a coffin in a mausoleum – *and she gets out*? The girl's my idol."

"When I suggested something more exciting I wasn't thinking of anything quite so radical," Tina said. "Just more exciting than paddling around in a pond like a bunch of twelve-year-olds. Like kayaking in the ocean. We could get close to those seals we saw from the beach yesterday. They were adorable, like chocolate labs, only wet."

"They're not amphibian dogs," Rachel said, "they're wildlife."

"You're not supposed to get close to them," Clare added. "Anyway, the water's too rough," "You're more likely to see your surfer dudes out in the ocean than kayakers."

"One year we should try it. Maybe the dudes give lessons." Clare looked in the rear view mirror and waited for Tina to make the expected remark about a possible exchange of lessons.

They passed another road leading to a second beach. "Didn't someone drown on that beach a couple of years back?" Rachel asked.

"You're just full of cheerful comments this morning," Tina said. "Did you weigh yourself today?"

"I remember that," Jane said. "We were all terrified it was you, Clare. You went for a long walk on the beach. We were this close to calling the police."

"I wasn't gone that long," Clare said.

"That's probably what the woman who drowned told her friends – *I won't be gone long*."

"All the more reason to go to the ponds," Clare said. "No waves, no undertow, no sharks, no serial killers. No need to channel our inner Ashley Judds."

"You're gonna make a great mom," Tina said, "you've already got that *because I said so* shit down pat." That elicited the first glimmer of a smile any of them had seen on Clare's face since the fruit basket arrived.

The road dipped and turned and soon the women saw slivers of water breaking through the solid wall of trees. Then the clearing and the boat ramp. Clare backed down the ramp as close to the water as she dared. Rachel and Jane stood on either side of the SUV undoing the bungee cords, loosening the tie downs and easing the first boat onto the soft sand near the water's edge. Once both kayaks were down and their gear unloaded, Clare pulled the car into a legal parking spot across the road.

The pond was actually three interlocking ponds with houses nestled in the trees, barely visible except for the telltale canoe or Sunfish pulled up on shore or attached to floating platforms where cormorants and herons sometimes rested. Rachel and Tina attached the kayak seats and backrests and Jane assembled the paddles.

"Feathered or not?" she asked.

"You always ask and I never know how to answer," Tina said. "I'm from Brooklyn, the City of Churches, not the City of Olympic kayakers. Does it really matter? It's not as if we're shooting the rapids."

"Plenty of kayakers in Jamaica Bay."

"I'm not one of them."

It did matter to Jane. She appreciated precision. That was the reason she enjoyed baking. It wasn't merely a talent she'd inherited from her mother. It appealed to her belief that if you followed instructions everything would turn out fine. She was the only person any of them knew who actually listened to the flight attendant when she gave her "in the event of an emergency" speech. She tossed a couple of PFDs to her friends and kept two for herself and Clare.

"Do we really have to wear these?" Tina said, "They

give you such weird tan lines."

Clare arrived in time to answer. "Absolutely. Put on self-tanner later if you don't want the funny lines. Everyone needs a personal flotation device – people can drown in as little as one foot of water."

Clare was either going to make a great mother or an incredibly neurotic one. Somehow they'd survived their own childhoods without every empty outlet plugged and every plastic dry cleaning bag and small part banished from their homes, but Clare's child would be protected from all such potentially lethal devices. Tina grumbled, taking one of the PFDs and filling the pockets with her idea of essentials – lip balm, sunscreen and her phone.

They divvied up the bottled water, wine and lunches and stowed them in the boats' hatches. If the water level was low they'd have to portage in between the ponds but with any luck they could simply get out and drag the boats through the channel and paddle to a private picnic spot they knew beyond the entrance to the third pond.

"Come with me," Rachel said.

"Only if you don't give me a hard time about my *Cleopatra on her barge* moments," Tina said.

"No problem, your highness. Let's take the green one. I have it on good authority the royal barges were not blue."

Clare and Tina each climbed into the front seat of a boat and settled in. As the stronger paddlers, Jane and Rachel took seats in the sterns and would handle the rudders. After adjusting their foot pedals and pushing off, Clare and Jane glided away first in the blue kayak, making the barest slice in the water. Clare trailed her fingers in the pond.

"Like a bathtub," she said, as Jane moved them out of the shallows.

"Probably colder in the middle where it's deeper. We're

lucky to get the house when we do. The weather is still beautiful and most of the summer people are gone."

"Summer people? Do you pretend to be local when you're here?" Clare asked.

"Not pretend, I try it on for size. What would my life be like if I'd made different choices? What would I do if I lived here? *If you lived here, you'd be home now.*" She recited the ubiquitous billboard message. "Everybody does that when they travel, don't they?

If Clare imagined a different life, she didn't share it. She had made choices. The biggest was leaving Brooklyn – her friends and family. Connecticut was hardly the Australian outback but at times it seemed just as foreign, and every once in a while she felt like letting loose with a well-timed "Fuggedaboudit!" if only to remind herself and her neighbors of who she was despite her mysterious new affinity for pearls and pastel clothing. She picked up her paddle just as Jane turned to look for the others.

"You guys okay back there?" she yelled.

Tina gave a thumbs-up. "Fine, I'm readjusting the foot thingy. Rachel's handling the heavy lifting. We'll catch up to you."

"Make sure that vest is on. It doesn't work as well if you leave it in your lap." Satisfied, Jane started paddling in earnest, putting her shoulders and torso into each stroke. She loosened her grip on the paddles and eased into a push and pull rhythm with her entire body. "Right now I'm pretending to be an Indian princess doing the silent paddle," she said, mostly to herself.

That was one of the pleasures of kayaking. The difficulty of hearing someone facing the other direction gave you license to benignly ignore them. Conversation trickled down to the bare essentials – *I'm taking a break. Want some water? Is that a heron?*

Clare fell into a regular rhythm and Jane timed her strokes. She always thought it incredibly graceful to see tandem paddlers in sync. There were few enough times people really were. She turned slightly to make sure Rachel and Tina had launched successfully and were in view. Rachel was a strong paddler but Tina was just as likely to stop suddenly and allow herself to drift through the lily pads powered by unseen hands like an empress on an imperial barge. That tendency had prompted the Cleopatra remark three summers earlier and it had stuck.

The blue kayak crossed the pond at a good pace, but slowly enough for the women to enjoy the occasional bird or patch of water lilies, which they tried not to disturb with their paddles. They found the passage – difficult to see unless you were close – through the waist-high reeds to the next bigger body of water, and the women used their paddles to push off from the sides and enter the second pond. Once they reached deep enough water, away from the bugs that swarmed around the shoreline, Jane stopped.

"Let's take a drink break and wait for the others," she said.

Clare nodded and rested her paddle on her thighs. When she twisted in her seat to get the water bottle, Jane saw she'd been crying. She leaned forward to squeeze her friend's shoulder through the bulky yellow life vest.

"C'mon, you're not still thinking about that stupid note, are you? I'm sure there's a reasonable explanation. Abby wouldn't do that to you. To any of us."

"I'm not worried about infidelity," Clare said. "Brian and I have already weathered that storm."

That snake. Jane had had her suspicions about Brian but never knew for sure. She wondered if the others did.

Clare nodded slowly. "Three years into our marriage.

An intern at the local public television station."

Freaking interns, Jane thought. What is it with them? Did Monica Lewinsky officially rewrite the job description to include ho-jos behind the file cabinets? Jane wondered how *she'd* react if Vincenzo cheated on her. Is a relationship ever the same after that kind of betrayal? Would she behave like some compliant politician's wife – forgive and move on?

"It's the baby," Clare said. "I don't think Brian wants it. Without a husband or the better paying job Abby was going to lie and say I held with her company we won't be able to adopt. I'm so tired of trying and not succeeding. I used to feel good about myself – crushed the SATs, magna cum laude, wedding announcement in the Times – now I feel like a failure at everything I do. All those years of not being able to get pregnant and all it got me were wildly fluctuating hormones, a sore ass and a floundering marriage. Maybe if I'd been able to conceive, I wouldn't have had the affair."

Jane was stunned at her friend's admission and silently apologized to Brian. Did that make Clare the snake? She knew it wasn't fair but, she didn't think so. When a man cheated he was a slime bag but when a woman did it, she must have had a reason? Right?

She was struggling to craft an appropriate response when they heard muffled shouts in the distance. Alone on the water they paddled as fast as they could back to the thin strip of land connecting the first two ponds. Jane climbed out and stood in the knee-deep water, shielding her eyes against the sun. What she saw created a knot in her stomach – the furious splashing of someone in the water and the upturned hull of a green kayak.

CHAPTER 6

A figure stood on a private floating dock on the opposite side of the pond. Clare squinted. "Is that Rachel?" she said.

"I can't tell," Jane said. "Let's get going." She climbed back into the kayak and readjusted her seat. "I'll power paddle, you try to keep up and tell me what you see as we get closer."

They shoved off in the direction of the overturned kayak which had drawn the attention of two or three onlookers on the far shore. A canoer hastily put in and headed for the same spot, but a swimmer was closest and would get there first.

"What's happening?" Jane said, not interrupting her paddling.

"The person on the dock isn't Rachel or Tina. She's pointing to a spot in the water."

The surface of the water was smooth as glass and Jane skimmed the kayak across the top without a wasted stroke. They were on a collision course with the canoe to get to the overturned boat where the swimmer had just dived under it, but the kayak with two paddlers was lighter and faster than the canoe, a heavier boat with one source of power.

"I can see Rachel! Just her head." Clare had to yell so Jane could hear her. "She's in the water to the left of the kayak."

"Where's Tina?" The wind had picked up and she had to keep paddling and handling the rudder or they'd drift off course. The wind blew her words away and Clare didn't hear her. Louder, she said, "Where's Tina?"

"I don't see her."

The swimmer dove again and this time the women were close enough to see the overturned kayak rocking violently in the water. The swimmer, a man, emerged with a limp, dark-haired figure that he held up by the waist and flung over the hull of the kayak. Despite being thrown against the bottom of the boat, the body didn't move.

The man guided the kayak to the floating dock with Tina draped across the hull and Rachel trailing behind, trying to push. Once they reached the private dock, the woman who'd first seen the mishap helped the swimmer drag a lifeless body onto the platform.

"Oh, my god," Clare said.

"What?"

"It's Tina! They're giving her CPR. She looks . . . she's not moving." Clare's sobs rocked the small boat.

"Stay calm. We're almost there."

By the time they were close enough to see, Rachel had heaved herself out of the water onto the dock. Two strangers were working on Tina.

When they reached the small dock, they stayed in their boat not wanting to crowd the floating platform. Rachel was on her knees, sitting back on her heels. She held her arms and rocked herself back and forth. She was still breathing hard. A bruise on her forehead was beginning to purple and strands of vegetation were stuck in her hair and on her watchband. Her PFD was gone.

"What the hell happened?" Jane said.

"Don't yell at me!" Rachel said, hyperventilating.

"I'm sorry. We're not yelling, honey."

"It all happened so fast." She gulped air. "Tina saw a box turtle and . . . wanted to take its picture with her phone. You know how close you have to get. She leaned over and I did too. Stupid. Then she started swatting at some Sikorsky-sized bugs and we capsized. I made the wet exit but Tina didn't get out. Maybe her foot got stuck. Maybe it was the straps on the vest. She didn't really put it on – she just draped it over her shoulders."

"And you let her?" Clare said.

"Thank you – I didn't feel bad enough before you said that."

"Calm down. Both of you," Jane said. "She's going to be okay." She hoped.

The man and woman took turns, continuing to push on Tina's chest and count. Jane watched and tried to remember what she'd learned in a YWCA lifesaving class, but now, when someone actually needed her it had all gone out of her head. *Tip the head back.* Maybe you could only stay that calm when it was a stranger on a gymnasium floor and not a friend turning blue. Luckily the couple who pulled Tina from the water remembered.

"I wasn't strong enough to flip the boat over." Rachel held her arms close, trying to control her breathing. "I couldn't go under with my life vest on, so I ripped it off. Once I was under . . ."

She shook her wet head so violently she sprayed the others with water. "We'd churned up so much dirt and sand I . . . I couldn't see. Then I got tangled in this stuff." Rachel picked at the green strands on her watchband. She started to whimper.

Clare tried to comfort her but from her seat in the kayak could only manage pats on her friend's knee.

"It's gonna be all right. Are you okay?" Jane said. "Your head . . . "

Rachel fingered the bump on her temple. "I must have hit my head on the boat when I dove under to get her."

The dock shook with the weight of two emergency medical technicians running from the shoreline. Just then, Tina belched up a lungful of water.

"Shit," she mumbled, water dribbling from the corner of her mouth. "I told you I didn't want to go kayaking."

CHAPTER 7

At the insistence of the EMTs, Tina was taken to the hospital, but refused to stay overnight. She touched her toes, walked in a straight line and answered so many questions she might have been auditioning for Jeopardy. Given that she was shamelessly flirting with the doctors and had three live-in nurses, she was deemed healthy enough to be released.

Once again, Tina was ensconced in the back of Clare's SUV with Jane looking after her. The mood was more subdued on the way back to the bungalow, Tina milking an "I-told-you-so" attitude that she'd make the others pay for the rest of the weekend. Clare parked on the sand outside their house and they walked single file on the narrow path cut through the sea grape. Before the screen door slammed Tina was in the kitchen looking for a drink.

"Well," she said, "you wanted an activity to take our minds off Abby's note. I wanted a little excitement. I'd say a near death experience qualifies as both." She hung on the refrigerator door searching for a Sam Adams.

Hunger hit them all at the same time. Half their picnic lunch had been lost to the ducks in the pond, but they broke out their one untouched hamper and pulled chairs around the picnic table on the bungalow's deck. From there they had a view of the dunes, the ocean and the edge of the deck of the house next door, to the right of theirs. They dug into soggy tuna sandwiches, cold beers and a tub of cole slaw brought from home.

"So," Tina said, "were you already planning what you'd wear to my funeral? Jane, you've got that nice Adrienne Papell."

"Too festive. I would have gone with my black suit."

"Every day?"

"Just how long an event are you expecting to have?"

"I don't know. Depends on whether it's before my book hits the bestseller list or after."

Her confidence was all for show. Deep down Tina knew most books came and went without causing a ripple, but it wasn't in her nature to not go balls-out, to drive herself as hard as possible and expect the best possible outcome. It was her "good Catholic work ethic," she'd explained. The first and only time her Catholicism had ever affected her behavior.

"If it's after," Jane said, "should we sell books?"

"Of course. Think of that poor bastard who wrote *A Confederacy of Dunces*. He didn't get famous until after he was dead."

"Is that a legitimate marketing strategy?"

"Only if all else fails."

They were still young enough to make cracks about death. It hadn't really touched them yet. Two of the women had lost parents – Rachel's dad and Jane's mom – but death was still something that happened after you were old and hobbled and preferably, they joked, after you'd buried several rich husbands. They could still eat and drink and stay up all night and look none the worse for wear the next morning. A few pounds were gained here and there and hair colors had changed numerous times, but that was elective and not yet a response to infiltrating grays. Apart from Clare's presumed infertility they were unabashedly healthy.

"Do you ever think about who will come to your funeral?" Rachel asked.

"No," Jane and Clare said in unison. "It's morbid," Clare added.

"I'll go to yours if you come to mine," Tina said, reaching for another beer. "I've already created a playlist. Classical mostly – and that song from *The Sound of Music* where they all say goodbye in different languages. I just hope I get a good crowd."

"I can bring the staff from Sweet Dreams if you like," Jane said. "To get your numbers up. Or we can call that gal who organized the reunion. She ought to be good for papering the house."

They tried to remember if they knew anyone their age who'd died.

"Richie Sapienza," Rachel said, after much thought. "Didn't he have some kind of fatal disease?"

"That was his pickup line," Tina said. "*Screw me now, I'm not going to see twenty-five.* Please don't tell us you fell for that."

"No, of course not," she said, uncomfortably.

"You did – I know that guilty look!"

"I didn't. But, that does explain a few things. I went to the park with him once and brought a bag of homemade rugelach and a copy of *Death Be Not Proud.*"

"Get out of here."

"Scout's honor," Rachel said. "My mother made me. She said it was a mitzvah. I thought Richie's reaction was weird but I just assumed he'd never eaten rugelach."

"Your mother's a trip," Tina said, shaking her head. "But in a good way."

They mentally trolled through their yearbooks and came up with two fatalities – one car accident on a lethal stretch of the Long Island Expressway and one drug overdose. The women hadn't been close to either of the victims, a studious boy with a fondness for sci-fi, and a pale skinny blonde who partied too much. Sad. To think of someone their own age, already in the ground.

"Well, I'm not going anywhere just yet," Tina said. "I've had two brushes with mortality recently – if you include that crazy broad in the Mercedes – and I'm still here. I intend to stick around for a while and have some fun while I do."

Her comment was inspired by the beer and possibly the renters next door who were noisily spilling onto their own deck. The women had seen them when they first arrived, three couples in their twenties with bodies unnaturally hard and hair annoyingly blond, the girls with beachy waves which Tina had once paid four hundred dollars for at a chichi downtown salon.

The previous year their neighbors had been a husband and wife in their seventies who went fishing out of Wellfleet Harbor every day and shared their catch – striped bass, bluefish, cod -with other residents on the short dirt road that led to the dune. The first time the couple knocked on their door with a giant bluefish Tina couldn't help but channel The Godfather. It was an Italian thing. A ritual family viewing of the entire three-part saga with commentary delivered by her father and brothers came shortly after her confirmation.

Before the older couple, there'd been a pair of gay guys

who kept to themselves except for the one night when they invited the women over for cocktails. Mars was close to earth, or Venus was in transit, Rachel would know, and the men had brought a telescope. Tina remembered only the bellinis and the picture perfect appetizers, not the astronomical occurrence.

But this year the neighbors were kids. Guaranteed to make the women feel like liver-spotted crones. There would be no shared food, no stargazing, and if the women didn't actively hate them, there was no love, only the slightly snarky comments of women who felt their twenties slipping further and further into the rear view mirror.

"She'll be sorry she didn't cover up more when she's paying a fortune to get those sun spots nuked," Tina said, peering over the shrub oak hedge. "And what she's got exposed is going to hurt like a mo-fo to get lasered."

"I haven't seen so many blondes in one place since Kate and I rented *Village of the Damned*," Rachel said.

The comments continued in that vein, each woman weighing in on the folly of youth and how genuinely glad they were not to be young and foolish anymore – until they heard a knock.

She of the notoriously small bikini and future melanomas stood alongside their deck. Jane hoped their strongest remarks hadn't been delivered when their visitor was within earshot.

Her teeth glowed white against her brown skin, the effect so dazzling it made Tina wince. The girl held an empty ice bucket against the impossibly long expanse of skin in between the two scraps of her swimsuit. She held out the bucket like a small child trick-or-treating or Oliver Twist requesting "more."

"Excuse me, ma'am. Ladies. Our ice maker isn't

working," she said. "Jared says it's appliance fatigue. He's gone to get some bags. He may have to go to New Orleans, but he's not from around here and he's been known to get lost. Can we borrow some to tide us over until he gets back?"

Borrow? Would they return the ice once they got drunk? And Jared may get lost? There was one road in and one road out of Wellfleet. The only way he could get lost was if he drove straight into the water. Jane could feel a scathing comment from Tina boiling up like the zinger she'd laid on the delivery boy. Jane snatched the bucket and led the girl to the relative safety of the kitchen. "Of course," she said. "What are neighbors for?"

"Awesome."

Tina shuffled behind them, as if observing a rare creature in the wild, while Rachel and Clare stayed outside, on the deck.

"Did we *ever* have asses like that?" Rachel whispered to Clare.

"If we did, we were so young only our doctors and our mothers saw them."

Jane used an empty plastic container to scoop up the ice cubes and fill the girl's bucket. As she waited the girl checked out their bungalow.

"This place is cool. Do you women own it?" The way she said it made Jane think she was in the "they must be gay" camp.

"We're just here for a long weekend," Tina said, trying unsuccessfully to hide her limp. The girl's eyes fell on Tina's rewrapped ankle, the hospital bracelet still on her wrist.

"Ziplining accident," Tina lied.

Then the girl saw the partially devoured fruit basket.

"Omigod! Did somebody die?" The concept seemed

even more foreign to Blondie than it had been to them. Death was something that happened in darkened movie theatres, not in real life. “I’ll tell my friends to keep the music down.”

“No, no,” Tina said, with a laugh. “The fruit basket is an inside joke. Don’t worry about the music. Actually we’re going out soon. There’s a new club on Route 6.”

“Sweet. What’s it called?”

Since there was no club, as least none that Tina knew of, she fumbled for an answer. The Lobster Lounge? Cranberry Crib? Ziplining? Jane saw through her friend’s feeble attempts to appear younger and hipper than she was.

“Yes, what was the name of that place?” she said, smiling.

“I forget the name. The renters from last year told me about it. It’s on one of those little roads off Route 6 on the way to Provincetown.”

If the fish folks from the previous year had indeed turned her on to a destination it would have been a senior center, a hospital or a bait shop. Jane handed the bucket to the girl and led her to the door. “Here you go. Don’t drink and drive.”

“Oh, no worries. I think we’re going to be staying in the house all weekend. But let us know about that club. All we’ve found is this redneck sports bar. I didn’t think there were rednecks in Massachusetts.” She trotted off, flapping her flip-flops, her photo-shopped butt swaying from side to side.

“You were awfully nice to her,” Tina said, once the girl left and they were back outside. “Was that absolutely necessary?”

“I was saving you from yourself.”

“She was eerie. Like the x-rated version of *Toddlers and Tiaras*. Is that redundant? I just didn’t expect a twenty-year-old ass to come waltzing into my celebratory, life-affirming meal.”

"Okay so she doesn't know the difference between Orleans and New Orleans unless Jared is even stupider and is really driving to Louisiana for ice."

"That's not what I meant. Did you see the junk in that trunk?"

Jane could hardly have missed it. The twins were exposed in all their glory separated only by a bit of red and white string that reminded her, disturbingly, of the twine she used at the bakery.

"Let's really go out," Tina said. "Otherwise we'll be over here listening to their music, playing Parcheesi and feeling like a bunch of geezers."

"Do you even know a place?" Jane asked.

"No, I made that up. Did you believe me?"

"Not for a minute."

CHAPTER 8

Rachel and Clare would have been perfectly happy to stay in and play board games, but Tina had capitulated on the kayaking and she convinced them that after what she'd been through they owed it to her.

A night on the town wasn't an activity they usually packed for on their long weekend, so they had to scrounge in their bags for suitable clothing. Any top with writing on it was eliminated, as were sneakers and baseball caps, which were fine for daytime and for younger girls at night but when you were on the far side of thirty looked like you were trying too hard. In the end they cobbled together four outfits, circulated the spray bronzer, piled into Clare's SUV and left in search of a good time.

They happily rejected the noisy family restaurants. What they wanted was music, and a few drinks, not all-you-can-eat clams and waiters dressed as pirates. After twenty minutes of driving the mood was less festive and they agreed to stop at a seafood joint, Captain Ahab's, which had a small bar near the take-out section. That summer the bartender was Latvian.

"Okay" Rachel said, as he walked away, "I've got nothing against *furr-iners*, but how do so many of them land jobs in Wellfleet? I wouldn't know the first thing about getting a summer job in the Balkans. How do they know Captain Ahab is *looking*?"

"Work/study visas," Clare said. "Must be an agency." She'd had experience with half a dozen foreign agencies for the adoption. Unlike Rachel, she probably did know how to get a summer job in the Balkans, or at least in Kiev.

Tina bought the first round at the Captain's and the women sampled the bartender's special mushroom appetizer, but after the second rendition of Happy Birthday from the dining room, complete with candlelit cupcakes, Tina begged them to leave.

In the parking lot she announced they were going to P-town.

"Tina, most of the bars in Provincetown are gay."

"We're not looking for lifetime commitments, just live music. Energy. Not exchange students hauling buckets of corn and steamers." She shifted her weight to emphasize her still-sore ankle, to remind them that she'd taken one for the team that morning and expected them to do the same that night. It worked.

They climbed into the car again and found nothing from Wellfleet to P-town that met Tina's requirements. The gay bars were too raucous and the local bars too depressing and the other women were losing interest in the pursuit. In the end, they settled for the redneck sports bar.

As the women pushed through the doors, a pinball machine buzzed, the Red Sox were on the tube, and the air was heavy with the smell of decades of spilled beer. Realizing this was her last option, Tina pronounced it perfect.

"I can be the designated driver tomorrow," Tina said.

"You mean you expect to come here twice in one weekend?" Rachel said, looking around the dingy bar. The walls were plastered with Boston paraphernalia, and posters and t-shirts offered helpful suggestions for where Yankees fans might go and what they might do.

"Don't be such a snob," Tina whispered. She hesitated between the bar and a cluster of empty tables. "Is there table service?"

The bartender nodded. "Eileen, you wanna help these ladies?"

Eileen was camped out at a table with a full ashtray, an empty beer glass and a spread out copy of the *Boston Globe.* In fact, she didn't look like she wanted to help them, but she hoisted herself out of the booth, and motioned to the tables with a gesture that said, *You need a freaking invitation?*

She followed the women to a table and stood, bored, waiting for their order. It was clear she would not be rattling off a long list of imported beers so the women quickly ordered three Sam Adams and a Diet Coke for Clare.

"I don't think she likes us," Rachel whispered, when the woman left.

Their drinks came and Tina took hers and a wad of singles from her bag. "Time for music."

Half a dozen, plaid-shirted men sat at the bar and Tina hobbled over to the jukebox, the cleanest, shiniest thing in the place if you didn't count the bartender's head. Within minutes, the youngest and best-looking of the men joined her where the other women heard her repeat the ziplining lie.

"It's uncanny," Rachel said. "She wants excitement, she gets it. She wants attention, she gets it." The others looked on.

"She may need to be rescued from this, too," Jane said.

Tina smiled. She flirted. Her new friend pointed to

something on the jukebox and set off a ripple of laughter before rejoining his pals at the bar. Tina smoothed and fed a few bills into the machine and a song the women knew and loved came on, so loud it shook the glasses behind the bar. Tina shrieked and started rocking on the sticky dance floor, standing in one spot, shifting her hips, not easy to do with one bum ankle.

"She's doing the hips and lips dance," Clare said. "Making orgiastic facial expressions. Like Mick Jagger."

"He had a band behind him. If he'd been doing it alone, he would have looked spastic. Kind of like Tina." Certain things done in a group were acceptable, even cool. But when done alone could be questionable. Think flash mobs. The wave. "Should we bail her out or let her keep embarrassing herself?" Jane said.

Tina wasn't the least bit embarrassed but was delighted and maybe a little relieved when the others joined her in a group dance, like they used to do to the boom box in Rachel's basement, improvised routines that had them sweating and collapsing in laughter until Rachel's mother came down and made them go home or go to sleep.

That night, Gilda Weiner wasn't there to impose a curfew and they didn't care if the flannel-shirted men at the bar did think they were two lesbian couples. Music, male attention (such as it was) and a few drinks. Mission accomplished.

After a dozen songs and two rounds of drinks, one purchased by a burly local who had a fondness for Rush and bore a strange resemblance to the truck driver from earlier in the day the women were back at the bungalow. A chill had set in so they layered on cheap fleece sweatshirts bought at one of the discount souvenir shops and Rachel built a fire, patiently layering twigs and other kindling until one match was all she needed to start the blaze.

"Bob teach you how to do that?" Clare asked.

Tina and Jane gawked; it wasn't like Clare to trash one of the husbands. Or anyone for that matter.

"What? I didn't mean anything. I don't know that I've ever made a fire in my own house. Brian always acts as if you need to have been an Eagle Scout to do it, so I always let him. Same with the damn gas grill."

"It was my mother," Rachel said. "She didn't like to leave stacks of newspapers near the fireplace. She'd invoke the Collyer brothers name every time we had more than three days worth of newspapers. This is nothing – Kate can make a fire with two sticks. And before you say it – one of them is not a match. She's the real Girl Scout, not me."

They unearthed dusty blankets from the linen closet and huddled around the small hearth on creaky wicker furniture. After the beers and the wine they hated their neighbor's music a little less. They toasted Gilda Weiner and Rachel for being good mothers and Tina for not being dead and brainstormed other ways to get her on the best-seller list since she'd lost out on the publicity-generating, fatal accident.

"I can't help it," Tina said. "I spent three years of my life writing that book and without some luck and a high-powered publicist I could be on the fast track to the bargain book table."

None of them really knew how publicity worked. Abby had helped Jane's business get off the ground, they'd attended her parties and celebrated her mentions in newspapers and magazines, but how their friend actually generated publicity was a mystery. They relived events and product launches and tried to visualize a comparable strategy for Tina.

By this time, Clare had gone to bed with a book. Rachel was snoring lightly. Tina got up, stumbled over to her handbag and held up a fabric pouch and dangled it in front of Jane's nose.

"You cannot be serious," Jane whispered.

"My brother Blaise gave it to me. He says it's primo stuff. No paranoia, minimal munchies." She pulled out two lumpy joints. "One for tonight and one for tomorrow. Should we wake Rachel or share this ourselves?"

"I'm not sleeping, I've been ignoring you," Rachel said, already sniffing the air. "But no matter what your brother says we're going to need more food. That mushroom appetizer was ages ago."

They passed the doobie and took turns telling stories at the expense of husbands, relatives, co-workers, ex-boyfriends and anyone else who'd ever done them wrong. The list wasn't particularly long and after two or three go-rounds they were reduced to resurrecting laughably minor slights, real or imagined, from high school and earlier.

Airing individual grievances was enormously cathartic – and an annual event. But this year it had the slightly frantic feel of people desperate to prove to themselves they were still young and hadn't a care in the world.

"You know what we're in, don't you?" Tina said, letting her breath and the smoke out in a rush. "We're in a donut hole. We're the forgotten demographic. Too old to be hipsters and too young to be – Helen Mirren. Companies don't even market to us anymore. Except for wrinkle cream and Singles in Your Area." Tina had crossed the line from happy and buzzed to something else.

This is why we never really did drugs, Jane thought. Not because we were such goody-goodies but because Tina would over-think and Rachel would over-eat and hate herself the following day.

But when they woke the next morning and surveyed the detritus they agreed the extra calories, under eye smudges and slightly fuzzy heads were worth it for the feeling of sisterhood and camaraderie their bacchanal had engendered.

For the rest of the weekend the women walked on the beaches, sunned themselves on narrow shorelines, hunted for beach glass and taste-tested Portuguese kale soup whenever they saw it on the menu. Rachel voted for Mac's. Jane was loyal to Blue Willow.

They visited every thrift shop on the Cape hunting for special bits of junk and spent so much time at the Wellfleet Flea Market people must have assumed they were vendors. They went to the movies twice, blockbuster films they'd ordinarily never have wasted their time on.

Tina acted as sommelier, opening the bottles early and often. Clare ran on the beach every morning and threw herself into their late-night Scrabble games, relishing her "spoiler" moves as much as she did her seven-letter words, which none of the others challenged since she was always right. One morning, Jane disappeared for hours, bicycling to every market in Wellfleet and Orleans looking for cream of tartar, then treated them to freshly baked scones topped with dollops of cranberry jam purchased at a roadside stand.

And on Sunday when it came time to close up the house, they declared the weekend a success and feigned regret at having to leave, but no one was really sorry. They stripped the beds, swept the sand from the rooms and brought the outdoor pillows into the sunroom with an enthusiasm suggesting they were leaving Shawshank prison, not a pricey rental on Cape Cod. Then they piled into Clare's SUV for the long trip back to Connecticut.

The drive from the Cape was not fun. People leaving a

vacation paradise were always more annoyed and annoying than those en route. And listening to the classic rock station didn't inspire the impromptu songfests and seat dances it had on the way up, so they turned off the music and drove with only the occasional recited billboard to break the silence until the rain started and the windshield wipers provided a monotonous, mind-numbing soundtrack to the journey.

Vacation mode was ending and if the issue of Abby's note wasn't exactly in the front of their minds it was no longer pushed to the back. Particularly if she didn't get in touch on Monday and offer an explanation. What did her note really mean? Where the hell was she? And with whom?

They sat near the entrance to the Sagamore Bridge, trapped in an endless line of traffic uselessly speculating about whether they should have left earlier or later before stopping for greasy food at a no-name diner that made the Wellfleet clam shacks seem like Michelin five-star restaurants. By the time they hit the road again, Tina and Rachel were nodding and Jane acted as co-pilot, her main job keeping the driver awake.

Rachel, Jane and Tina would drive to Brooklyn in Rachel's car, still parked in Clare's garage. Later in the week, Kate would return from a basketball tournament in upstate New York and Gilda from her casino outing. Then Rachel and her daughter would head back to the wilds of Pennsylvania to wait for Tomato Bob to trek out of the Utah wilderness.

The fall term wouldn't start for a week so Tina would write or more likely spend hours online indulging in games of chance, social media porn, and doing research that would never see its way into the next book. And she'd wait for David.

Jane would open her shop in the wee hours to bake muffins and cookies and slowly make the change from her summer to fall menu. And wait for Vincenzo. And eventually they'd all find out if the fifth Bitch's note was for real or just a joke that had unintentionally and painfully hit home.

At Clare's, the four friends said their goodbyes, each wondering what the circumstances of their next meeting would be. Would they be celebrating? Consoling? Laughing that they'd taken Abby's joke seriously – which they'd all vigorously deny doing? Most important – would anyone be missing?

CHAPTER 9

Clare and Brian Didrikson lived in Winston Heights, in a two-bedroom, California contemporary, about fifty years old, built into the side of a rock ledge. Skylights and sliding glass doors let in lots of light, and the open floor plan made the house feel bigger than it was. There was only one functioning bedroom, the smaller second bedroom having been quietly converted into an office/storage room as time went on and the hoped-for blessed arrival failed to arrive.

A separate outbuilding stood behind the house where Brian had installed an edit suite – a show-of-faith wedding present from his in-laws. He'd been working on his one video project since the day the couple met at WHCT, the television station where she'd been development director and he an assistant producer. She felt quietly proud whenever she had the chance to say that her boyfriend and then husband, was a filmmaker. But after so many disappointments and false starts she found it hard to stay optimistic. Neither of them was successfully producing and their individual failures were beginning to form cracks in their relationship.

Brian was attractive, in a boyish, used-car-salesman kind of way, with a ready smile and a winning manner. Colleagues at the station assumed he was on the fast track. Clare's mother instantly adored him, and while that would send many daughters sprinting in the opposite direction, the mother had read the tea leaves favorably for Clare's older sister, Laura, now disgustingly happy, married to a hedge fund manager with whom she'd borne three disgustingly cute, if somewhat hyperactive, children. They'd just moved into an eight-thousand-square-foot, seven-bedroom home in Dutchess County, which Clare alternately lusted after and was repelled by.

She wasn't jealous, but once she visited her sister's new palace, her own home felt cramped. The house was fine for empty-nesters or perhaps a gay couple with no children, she'd said, suggesting to The Bitches she and her husband were considering trading up, but it wasn't true. At least they weren't in the foreseeable future.

Clare found herself thinking about her sister's house over and over again. The accumulations of eight years of marriage had filled the small Didrikson home to excess. More than once she and Brian had argued about hanging pots and china cabinets, things she thought made a home a home but he dismissed as useless dust collectors. Appliances were starting to break down. They'd bought the house with all the regulation equipment – refrigerator, dishwater, stove and the like. If you had blindfolded Clare and asked their brand names she wouldn't have been able to identify them. But now that they had to be replaced she found herself being seduced by ranges that cost as much as her first car and refrigerators that gleamed like space capsules.

Was the need to refurnish hard-wired into every

woman's DNA or just hers? Was that another reason she was so obsessed with the adoption – new rooms to fill, new things to buy? New departments to shop in? Was it the seemingly universal need for more and bigger or was it a different vacuum she was trying to fill?

Once, early in the adoption process, Clare casually mentioned turning the studio into a room for the baby when she became a teenager and that created a new wave of tension between them. Brian insisted he'd have a production deal before the kid – who hadn't even arrived yet – became old enough to need "her own place" and Clare regretted bringing it up. It had made her feel disloyal.

When all the goodbyes were said, she entered the house through the garage the way she usually did, kicking off her shoes in the mud room and slipping into the black Merrells she kept by the door. She dropped her bags on the banquette in the kitchen, pointedly ignoring the flashing message light on her house phone. Anyone who knew her would have known she'd been away and would have called the cell if it was something urgent. The "important message" from her cable company and her party's candidate could wait and she wasn't ready for another message from Brian. What would this one be? An address where she could send his things? She'd need a good night's sleep before she could deal with that.

If he had left her, she had no right to be upset. She'd come close to confessing all to Jane in the kayak and might have if it hadn't been for Tina's accident. Clare had humiliated Brian. And with a college kid. Everyone at the television station knew. An intern from Yale. Brash, privileged, and unable to keep his mouth shut about a spontaneous encounter in Clare's office. It was not a drunken office party which might have been understood if not condoned, but it had taken place with all the lights on and others still in the building. It was shockingly brazen and left Clare profoundly embarrassed. She was forced to resign. Since they couldn't both quit their jobs Brian stayed on. The injured party. The cuckolded husband. Could she be surprised if she'd pushed her husband to the edge? Into the arms of a more supportive woman? Well, let someone else try it for a while. Easy to be supportive from the sidelines. A lot harder when you lived it day in and day out.

Clare wasn't proud of what she'd done, but as she packed the contents of her office after her sudden resignation and the intern's redeployment, she felt a twinge of something strangely like pride. *I'm not who you think I am. I'm not dried up and done.* Only after, did she feel regret.

Her shoulders were stiff from the long drive. All she wanted was a steaming hot Jacuzzi and a glass of something stronger than the light white wine and beer she'd mechanically sipped all weekend.

An hour later, wrapped in a thick white terry robe, Clare entered her family room and stood before the same credenza her book club acquaintance had attacked when delivering the news that her husband had left her. Perhaps as had been suggested, bad news went best with one beverage.

Brian fancied himself a connoisseur of quality scotch but to Clare it was all the same – something men imbibed to set themselves apart from the beer drinkers. She poured an inch of Brian's favorite into a heavy-bottomed rocks glass, and then added another inch for good measure. *Why did people like this stuff?* Just inhaling the smoky aroma was enough to give Clare a buzz but she steeled herself and took a throat-scorching sip before turning on the television to watch the news.

She stretched out her long, slim legs on the soft leather

ottoman in front of her. She'd been scrupulous about researching kid-friendly furniture ever since they'd started making plans for a family. Nothing with hard edges – the glass coffee table Brian thought so sophisticated in his post-grad apartment in Astoria had been banished to his studio. He'd grumbled that the small space was overcrowded but acquiesced when he realized the alternative for the table was a one-way trip to Goodwill.

Clare twisted her torso to give herself a good stretch. Two on each side, left, right. One more time. The second swallow of scotch went down easier than she expected. Maybe Brian and her old book club friend knew something she didn't. She filled the glass again before hunkering down on the sofa under a brown chenille throw.

The trifecta of the six hour drive, the warmth of the blanket and a tumbler of scotch had made Clare drowsy. Her head listed to one side and she propped it against the artfully arranged stack of throw pillows that had once been the ridiculous flashpoint for another argument with Brian. Was that a legitimate reason for desertion – irreconcilable decorating differences? She burrowed deeper into the sofa instead of dragging herself upstairs to the bedroom where she'd be conscious of being the only occupant in the queen-sized bed, and she'd stay awake, staring at the ceiling and wondering what was going to happen tomorrow – would one of her friends would be the recipient of bad news? Tina perhaps, who joked that she didn't care but who would be crushed if David left her. Or Jane, with her handsome Italian lover, who she only intermittently wanted to marry. Or would it be as she feared? She hit the remote to turn down the volume on the television and surfed for the comfort of an old black-and-white film or the familiar sight of Mariska

Hargitay and her scowling partner promising earnestly that everything would be all right.

And she drifted off before seeing the report of a woman's body found at a local train station.

CHAPTER 10

Vincenzo and Marco Palmieri had immigrated to the States while a third, much older brother Renzo, remained in Italy. Vincenzo planted his roots less than an hour from where their plane had landed, but Marco kept going west – all the way to Los Angeles where he became a fashion stylist. His job paid well and the perks included invitations to A-list events on both coasts, including a book launch planned by Abby Daniels. That was where Jane had met the brothers.

She didn't fall for Vincenzo right away. That was not her style. It took more than one look at a pretty face to set her back on her heels. It took a whole week. And even then she didn't sleep with him. She hired him.

Vincenzo was a pastry chef, Jane's first full-time employee joining Mo Heedles and a handful of other part-timers at Sweet Dreams. He worked alongside her for three months and when she felt confident enough in his abilities to promote him to overnight baker she looked forward to sleeping in until a sloth-like 5:30 a.m., or what her momma would have called dark-thirty. But with the same anxiety a new parent must feel when leaving her child with a babysitter for the first time, Jane couldn't relax and at 4:15 a.m. the first morning he was scheduled to open by himself she got dressed and headed for the bakery.

He had asked if it was all right to bring an iPod and portable speaker into the bakery while he worked and she didn't see the harm in it as long as he didn't wear ear buds which might interfere with his hearing the timers go off. Still she was surprised when she arrived and heard the clear, round tones of Luciano Pavarotti singing schmaltzy Italian love songs. She didn't know what she'd expected, but it wasn't that.

When Jane entered the kitchen, it was as hot as the tropics. Vincenzo must have gotten there extra early, anxious to get a good start on his debut as a keyholder. Jane liked that. He wore what some people called a wifebeater – a name she detested even more than the one Glenn Buonofiglio used – a guinea tee. When Vincenzo had applied for the job, she could, of course, see the dark good looks and affecting smile but his body was well-hidden by the bulky leather jacket and loose v-neck sweater underneath. That night, in his skinny tee nothing hid the well-defined arms, toned abs and what The Bitches would have called the perfect distribution of chest hair – at least what Jane could see of it.

With his longish hair pulled into a stubby ponytail Jane was briefly nervous about being alone with him. Not that he would try anything, but that she'd be caught staring at him with something more than managerial interest. You knew a guy was hot when he could rock a hairnet.

She'd peeled off her jacket, put up her hair and went to work alongside him. In addition to her regular breads and staples, the specials that morning were almond croissants, carrot muffins and one of her mother's favorites – red velvet cupcakes. They were recipes she knew by heart and it was a good thing because she spent most of the time surreptitiously watching him.

After a few weeks they dropped the pretense of his needing direction or her being unable to sleep and it was a given they'd be spending the night together listening to old Italian songs like *Parla mi d'amor* and falling in love while chopping nuts, grating carrots and mixing egg wash.

Jane thought of those early days as she raised the iron security gate and turned the key in the front door at Sweet Dreams. She pulled down the gate behind her and closed the door. It was not quite five a.m. and she already felt behind. Luckily, they kept emergency batches of cookie dough and cupcake batter in the freezer, a tip she picked up from the co-owner's mother, Ann-Marie Buonofiglio.

In the past the emergency batches had been used when Jane and Vincenzo were such a new couple they couldn't bear to leave their bedroom or keep their hands off each other. These days, it was more likely because Vincenzo had been taking special catering gigs and their schedules were no longer as regular as they'd once been.

Abby had been responsible for the most lucrative jobs, recommending him to some of her high-profile clients. Early on he'd go straight from an evening event to the bakery, dragging his ass but needing the money and not wanting to disappoint either woman. Jane had squeezed a love seat into the tiny office so that one of them could nap while the other worked, but more recently Vincenzo had gone home alone.

She stashed her bags and went through her routine, twisting her hair into a long rope, putting it in a clip and scrubbing her hands. She went to work. At 6:01 a.m. the phone rang. What time was it in Italy? 12 p.m.? 1p.m.? She never got that right. Vincenzo would know she was in the bakery. Maybe there *had* been an emergency. Even families that weren't close circled the wagons when bad times struck. She peeled off one plastic glove and answered the phone.

It was her partner, Glenn Buonofiglio, asking her to marry him.

CHAPTER 11

"Hey, dollface. How ya doin'?"

"Hi, Glenn."

"What's goin' on? What's the good word?"

With Glenn Buonofiglio there were many versions of *hello* before any actual content was exchanged. At six a.m. what did he think was going on?

"Nothing much, Glenn. Just sitting around reading the bible."

"You're such a kidder. I know you. You're probably working like crazy. My mother said you were a keeper."

Then it came. Like clockwork.

"When you gonna make us both happy and be my bride? My mother's been stockpiling Jordan almonds ever since she met you."

His proposals came about once a month, like her period, although the two didn't seem to be synchronized and this one was delivered with a little less enthusiasm than usual. Maybe his affection was waning. Or maybe at that hour, he was simply hung over and delivering the message by rote.

"I'm sorry, Glenn. No can do, I have a busy day. Look, the timers are going off, I'm going to have to cut this short." The marriage proposals aside, Jane liked to remind Glenn theirs was a business relationship.

"So what's goin' on with you?" she said, slipping into his vernacular. "You and Jimmy want to see the books?"

"All work makes Jane a dull girl. Nah – it's not business. Listen, I stopped in late Saturday and Mo reminded me you were away. I just called to see how your big girlfriends' weekend went. You know, one of these days I could come with you. Be your driver. Just me, and the rest of you. There's what – five of you? Madonna mia! We could have pina coladas and get lost in the dunes – like that song."

This was not an image Jane wanted etched in her brain all day and now that stupid tune would be an earworm, in permanent rotation on her internal soundtrack until something else replaced it. She did not want to *Escape* with Glenn Buonofiglio. He was sweet, good-looking and undoubtedly some women would have been flattered to have such a persistent suitor, but Jane Monaghan was not one of them.

"I'll ask the gang," she said, "and get back to you."

He mumbled something about an upcoming party and Jane agreed he should stop by the bakery sometime that week to discuss.

The locals in Jane's Brooklyn neighborhood had all known Ann-Marie Buonofiglio's Stromboli Shop was in trouble. The once-full shelves and deli cases still held carnival glass cake stands and decorative plates, but they were increasingly bare or covered with dusty paper doilies and rock-hard pignoli cookies left over from the weddings of customers who were now the parents of toddlers.

Ann-Marie had hoped her son would join her in the business and eventually take over but he was frequently called away on construction jobs. At least that was the shorthand she used, which didn't invite further inquiry. That had been hard on Ann-Marie – and her business – because the midnight deliveries of almond paste and other expensive ingredients, astonishingly enough, stopped coming once he went away.

Besides, the neighborhood was changing. There were just so many sfogliatelle anyone could eat in a week. Or a lifetime. Her clientele was literally dying off and was not being replaced.

Jane patronized the place because she had a soft spot for independent, female-owned businesses. Or maybe Ann-Marie resurrected childhood memories of Jane's own mother, her hands and hairline faintly dusted with flour or powdered sugar. Or maybe because a window seat was always available and Ann-Marie never pushed her to leave or order more and kept the strong, hot coffee coming. So Jane went to the bakery every morning with her laptop, job-hunting and hoping she was helping the place look solvent.

Jane had been a fit model and had enjoyed the work, but it failed to lead to a job with a fashion magazine or upscale retailer. And if she admitted it, even though hers wasn't runway work, she felt modeling was a job for a younger woman. Not that a wrinkle or two would have stood in her way as long as her proportions remained the same, but she had seen it all before and was losing interest in whether wide or cigarette leg pants would be in fashion next season. And every year a new crop of girls came along who cared passionately one way or the other. So she resigned. Her mother's passing had given her a monetary cushion, just enough to let her feel she could make a career change without worrying that she'd turn into a bag lady.

One morning at the shop, trolling through employment websites, Jane heard a cry and the clatter of aluminum trays crashing to the floor. She ran behind the counter and into the kitchen where she found Ann-Marie Buonofiglio sprawled on the floor and partially glazed with a light golden cream. The heavy vat she'd been trying to lift must have put her off-balance and sent her careening into a rack of empty baking sheets and coating the unconscious woman's face. All she needed were sprinkles.

By the time the ambulance arrived, Ann-Marie had regained consciousness and had extracted a promise from Jane to keep the shop open while she recovered or at least until Glenn returned from his latest job. It was a paying job and she wouldn't starve. Jane took the keys.

That first day managing the shop, mindlessly watching the foot traffic passing but not coming in, Jane counted two dozen women about her age on their way to Gymboree or wherever they were going, pushing Transformers-like carriages, cell phones glued to their heads, tiny purebred dogs on long leashes trailing behind them. Standing by the front door she overheard a snatch of conversation. *Play dates.* Large groups of women and kids.

They couldn't *all* be eating gluten-free foods and prewashed baby carrots.

That night, back in her fifth floor walk-up, Jane unearthed her mother's recipe box, the same sticky wooden box with the resin flower decorations she remembered her mother taking out every night after dinner when Jane went to her room to finish her homework. The recipes for Jane's favorites were torn out of magazines and newspapers and clipped together or handwritten in tiny, careful script on index cards faded with time or covered with brownish red stains.

Lady Baltimore cake, pecan tartlets, almond crescents and no fewer than three recipes for the red velvet cake, which Jane hadn't had for years lest she go up a size. Her mother's southern roots showed in her baking but almost nowhere else except for the sweet tea that she drank gallons of and forbade Jane to touch since it was probably spiked.

The next day Jane brought iced cookies and cupcakes to Ann-Marie's store. They sold. She put a doggie water bowl outside and placed a jar at the counter with homemade dog biscuits. Later that week she stood outside the shop in a crisp white apron and handed out mini-cupcakes to whomever would take them, mostly toddlers who stood rooted to the spot wailing until their mothers got off their phones and determined it was okay to take the treat from the nice lady. By the end of the second week, she'd mastered the shop's ovens and installed timers and had special orders for two children's birthday parties.

After six months with Glenn still out-of-town and the bed-ridden Ann-Marie urging her to become a partner, Jane began to give it serious thought. The catering business was going well and the espresso machine that had miraculously materialized after a casual conversation with one of Ann-Marie's many nephews had turned the place into a pleasant afternoon destination with a group of regular customers. And she liked the environment. All day long she was surrounded by happy people. People who were treating themselves or others instead of colleagues who were cranky, back-stabbing and starving themselves.

It was decided. Jane would use some of her savings to invest. Ann-Marie Buonofiglio, who had moved to Trenton, New Jersey to be cared for by her sister, would be a long-distance advisor. And her son Glenn, who had since returned, assumed the role of business partner, which he seemed to think meant taste-testing the products and occasionally arriving with a group of friends he encouraged to shop freely. Soon after, thanks in part to her mother's old recipes, and Abby Daniels coming up with a new name, the Stromboli shop was reborn as Sweet Dreams.

Then Abby had introduced her to Vincenzo.

CHAPTER 12

His credentials were from a cooking institute in Sicily that Jane had never heard of and couldn't find online, but that didn't trouble her. Word of mouth was everything and he'd gotten glowing references from Abby and numerous caterers who'd hired him as pastry chef for private corporate parties. Vincenzo was *creative, careful and responsible.*

No mention was made of just how fine he looked with an apron tied low and tight around his slim hips or how strong and capable his hands and arms were as they lifted heavy sacks of flour and tubs of fresh butter. And the way the faint sheen of perspiration made him look like a model in an underwear ad – minus the vacuous expression.

Three years into their romantic relationship, when Jane learned that two of her customers were engaged she flipped the Open sign to read Closed, locked the door and inexplicably burst into tears. She insisted to Mo and Shanika it was hormonal, but when Vincenzo heard about it, like a perceptive and loving partner he popped the question, making her a ring out of a lump of cookie dough.

She didn't hold him to his cookie dough promise. If

they did marry one day she didn't want it to be because of her biological clock, his sense of duty or because "coffee and a sticky bun" and "mini-muffin with tea, please" were getting hitched.

So they hadn't married. She'd sprayed the cookie dough ring with acrylic from an arts and crafts store and put it in her jewelry box absolving Vincenzo and telling him with a laugh that they'd do it when the time was right. He hadn't asked again. Vincenzo fell into referring to Jane as his woman. And he was *her man*. The same phrase used in Abby's fruit basket note.

The story of the cookie dough wedding ring got around though, and maybe that was what inspired Glenn Buonofiglio. His first day back in town he came to meet the woman his mother had described as a real catch – even if she wasn't Italian – and like a good son he popped the question. Jane was fairly sure his proposals were a running joke, his way of saying he wanted to stay involved in the business, and his asking and her saying no became a harmless habit they'd fallen into.

The bakery's accountant was a wizened Yoda-like man with big ears and Coke-bottle glasses named Jimmy Sicigniano. He'd shuffle in periodically in his cheap cardigan and brown jacket which probably fit him once but no longer did and ask to see "da books." He'd been handling the Buonofiglio family's finances since the days when Ann-Marie's mother sold charlotte russes and took bets from the back of her father's ice truck. Every time Jimmy came into the bakery, Jane held her breath, afraid that he'd expire right in front of the cookie counter where a group of children stood, traumatizing them for life – and worse still – putting them off baked goods.

In fact he moved pretty well for a guy pushing ninety,

but both Ann-Marie and Glenn were dead serious when they instructed Jane to not refer to him as *spry*. She never asked why and was always tempted whenever he visited, just to see what would happen, but his tough-talking granddaughter, Roseanne, a stick-thin girl with a huge head of black hair sometimes escorted him, and she looked like she could happily beat the living crap out of Jane. Roseanne also let it be known that she would find out if Jane tried any "funny business" with Glenn, who she'd decided was the only man for her. Yet another reason to give the woman – and Glenn – a wide berth.

It was explained to Jane that for tax and health insurance purposes, Glenn would, at least on paper, be listed as the co-owner instead of Ann-Marie. It was fine with Jane, especially since a steady stream of Glenn's friends came in the shop on Sundays when, in an unofficial homage to Ann-Marie, Jane offered Italian delicacies, which the older woman had taught her to make over many collect calls made from the Jersey shore.

From her office in the back of the bakery, Jane sensed more than heard movement in the shop. Then came the sound of the front gate being rolled up – the rusty hinge Vincenzo had never gotten around to scraping and oiling. Hadn't she put down the gate? Yes, but she hadn't relocked it. That was stupid.

No one else was scheduled to be in that early. Mo came on at eight and Shanika at three to deal with the breakfast and afterschool crowds. Jane tiptoed out of her office toward the sounds, gripping her offset spatula as if it were a weapon – not terribly useful unless the intruder was a fly. She spotted a better one. Should she announce herself or stay hidden?

She peeked around the corner behind the glass-front

counter. In the half-light of the early morning she saw the back of a rounded, crouching figure near the blue glow of the refrigerated beverage case.

"Hello!" she said. "We're not open yet . . . "

The figure rose and spun around to face her, a large expanse of fabric flying around. "Jeez, don't you have any diet Dr. Brown's?" Tina Ruggiero never knew how close she came to being brained with a marble rolling pin.

"What the hell are you doing here?" Jane said. "And don't you *knock*?"

"The gate was unlocked. I didn't realize you'd be *armed*."

"What are you doing here?"

"I knew you'd be working, but I couldn't bring myself to tell you over the phone," Tina said. "Clare called me two hours ago."

"Is she all right?"

"Yes . . . but . . . " A buzzer went off and Tina jumped. Jane checked her watch and headed for the kitchen, her friend trailing behind.

"You shouldn't be in here dressed like that. Hair. Fuzz. That's all I need – mohair in the muffins. Give me eight minutes and I'll meet you in my office."

Eight minutes seemed a little nitpicky, but then she remembered that Jane answered to a series of timers and one minute either way could mean trashing an entire tray of cookies for being underdone or too brown around the edges. Tina silently thanked heaven that her own actions never required such precision.

In exactly eight and a half minutes Jane entered her office, peeling off her silicone gloves and pulling off her hairnet.

"Four dozen mini-muffins, two dozen almond croissants and four dozen leaf-shaped cookies, cooling and waiting to be decorated even as we speak. Are you here to help?"

Tina shook her head. "Anything more difficult than pushing the chocolate kiss into the center of a warm peanut butter cookie is above my pay grade. I'd be big as a house if I was around stuff like that from morning until night."

"You get used to it," Jane said. "What's the latest?"

Clare had called earlier that morning. Tina had been wide awake. She said she'd had an epiphany about her novel and wanted to get on the computer before she fell asleep and the inspiration evaporated. It was also possible she was online in the wee hours yakking with strangers, something she denied doing but felt she had to with the book coming out. Building her platform she called it.

Clare had come home to a voicemail message she had assumed was from Brian. She didn't want to listen to it until the morning, but woke up on her sofa at three a.m. and decided what the hell, if it's bad news, it's bad news, so she played it.

"She stewed about it for a while, then tried to instant message me," Tina said, "but she phoned when she saw I was online."

"Working on your social media?"

Tina got defensive. "Being online is work. Anyway, the message was from Abby's assistant. The new, weasly one. Abby never showed up for her last appointments. He thought Clare would know where she was."

"Did he say anything else?"

"Just that she had cancelled her entire afternoon. She saw her trainer in the morning, had a breakfast meeting, then swung by the office to pick up a few things. He saw her climb into a car and thought it was business as usual until two clients called about rescheduling. He didn't know anything about it and couldn't reach Abby so he figured she decided to go to the Cape with us instead of meeting us there. That's when he left the message for Clare but by then we were already gone."

The assistant could have called any of them. Why Clare? Did he suspect something? Then something else dawned on her. Had he called Clare because she was the *safe* one to call? Just then a second realization shook her. Beyond the shock of losing Abby as a friend, if Abby *had* run off with one of their men, almost all of them would be affected in other significant ways. Until that moment it hadn't yet registered that a break with Abby might affect Jane's livelihood. Was it supremely selfish to be thinking in those terms when one of her closest friends might be headed for heartbreak?

"Okay, I'm a bitch," she said. Sheepishly, she told Tina what she'd been thinking.

"You are not a bitch," Tina said. "A *real* bitch would have thought of it three days ago. Like I did."

CHAPTER 13

By the time she turned thirteen, Tina Ruggiero had perfected the sullen facial expression and insouciant body language that said – like the little boy in the Maurice Sendak books – "I don't care."

She grew up with three older brothers, Blaise, Brent and Benedetto – Tina's name was short for Bettina. Her attitude had been a defense mechanism against the boys and their teammates and friends who filled the Ruggieros' semi-attached, brick home with testosterone, relentlessly teasing and tormenting the girl until her thirteenth birthday. Then the tables miraculously turned. The jokes stopped. The insults stopped. Boys were clumsy and tongue-tied in her presence. The tormented became the tormenter. All at once the "I don't care" pose served another purpose.

Growing up around so many men had given Tina a confidence and ease with the opposite sex not many teenage girls enjoyed. And she could launch a perfect spiral; it was the rare head cheerleader who could throw a pass as well as deflect one. That and her go-to expression made her one of the coolest girls in school. And to some, a bitch.

This same quality also made her fearless, had given her the courage to try acting as a profession and later, had made her think she could simply decide to write a potboiler novel and do it. It was also the quality that made David Handleman fall crazy, stupid in love with her.

When he met Tina, her first short story had just been published. She was aglow with the anticipation of future successes but not to the extent that she retired her "I don't care" posture. If anything, writers needed tough skins as much as actors and younger sisters did.

Tina's story had been included in an anthology edited by one of David's colleagues, and friends and family of the authors had gathered in a musty, independent bookstore to drink inexpensive wine and nibble hunks of Costco cheese thoughtfully provided by the small press that released the collection. Rachel, Clare and Jane had been there to fly the colors and show their support.

Abby, who'd been traveling, sent a flower arrangement and a jeroboam of champagne, an over-the-top acknowledgment for a minor contributor whose name wasn't even on the cover of the book, but it had made Tina feel like a real writer and she never forgot the gesture. She still had the bottle. It sat dusty, sticky, and empty on a shelf above her refrigerator holding up a stack of never-used cookbooks, still waiting for its mate which would arrive when Tina's first novel was published the following spring. At least that was the plan.

Once or twice Tina had speculated that if Abby had attended the book party that night, *she* and David might have gotten together. Not permanently. Just long enough to ruin him as a possible date or mate for the rest of the group. The Bitches never knowingly commingled their male conquests – at least not until this weekend. As far as Tina knew, it had only happened once before. By accident. And only two of them knew about it.

But Abby *hadn't* been at the book launch and David moved in with Tina shortly after her second feature article sold – a humorous, long form piece for a woman's blog that led to a lunch date with an editor and the suggestion that Tina flesh it out and turn it into a novel, which she did, the soon-to-be-released potboiler.

The rights had been licensed in what her agent referred to as "a very nice deal," not enough to retire on but encouraging enough to send Tina back to her computer to work on a second novel before the first had hit the shelves. That she had started writing later and had gotten published first was something of a sore point between the couple, but David was tremendously proud of his wife and most of the time theirs was a healthy competition.

People always said write what you know, but having plumbed all her life experiences, and then some, for her debut novel about the young teacher, Tina was breaking new ground for her sophomore effort. This would be a departure for her. Something darker. What she had yet to share with most of her friends was that she was writing the story of a young woman who attends a reunion and is not who she seems.

CHAPTER 14

Sitting in the still-closed shop, the light barely filtering in through the half-raised gate, Tina sucked down diet Dr. Brown's while Jane filled the display cases with freshly-baked goods.

"It's gotta be Brian," Tina said.

"Not that again."

Abby Daniels was their friend. Yet, if they were honest, they'd all just spent days questioning that relationship. She'd been the last to join their circle and the first to leave, if they counted that summer after high school graduation when she'd gone to Africa with her father. Tina pelted Jane with observations and recollections that showed Brian as the likeliest candidate for adultery.

"You can't do that," Jane said. "You can't go back twenty years and look for every instance of questionable behavior. Besides, we'll know soon enough and then you'll feel foolish for having indulged in these crazy theories."

"Good. That's what I hope. I'll put them all in the next book. But in the meantime, where the hell is she?"

"I have to open." Jane turned the lights on, started the

coffee and plugged the shop's iPod into the speaker system. It was her habit to start each morning with Bill Withers singing "A Lovely Day" and continue with positive, cheery songs throughout the day. Some of her customers even remarked that her playlist sent them out the door smiling.

Within thirty minutes the small bakery was filled. Students needing an espresso fix. Ruddy-faced children, none of them ruminating over calorie counts. Stay-at-home mothers cradling the latest additions to their growing families. When Mo arrived, Tina and Jane let her take over.

"That could be us," Tina whispered to Jane, watching the mothers from afar.

"I hate to be the bearer of bad news but they're a lot younger than we are. Our generation started late. We wanted to accomplish things before we had babies. At least that's what we said – I don't know that we did."

"I blame Brittany Spears," Tina said. "She started this baby boom. Before that, were baby bumps the latest accessory? Did that expression even exist?"

"I think it was referred to as "a bun in the oven," Jane said. "The mound itself didn't have a name."

Tina softened as an adorable toddler named Scarlett color-coordinated the sprinkles on her cupcake. "They are awfully cute though. Have you ever seen sneakers that small?"

Just then the shriek of a toddler ripped through the air. Tina cupped her ears.

"On the other hand, teaching has given me quite enough of kids for the next few years. That and spoiling my nieces and nephews rotten. My mother is getting impatient but I've told her if she asks me *the question* one more time she won't see me until Christmas. We know Clare's position on motherhood. What about you?"

Tina gestured around the bakery. "Is this enough of a kid fix for you? Feed them a lot of sugar and then send them on their way?"

Jane was noncommittal. "The shop is my baby."

"That's the way I feel about my book. I figure we have fifteen years before we'd need to join a support group for Older Pregnant Women," Tina said. "Used to be fifty-year-old moms who made the *National Enquirer*. Now sixty is the cut-off. Rachel was lucky to have Kate when she did. Even if the circumstances weren't optimum. Statistics show she'd probably be divorced anyway by now – so what if she did things out of order."

"You're so lucky with Vincenzo," Tina said, softly. "Handsome, talented, never has to wear suits or worry about someone else getting the promotion." Tina sounded exhausted, as breathless as if she'd run a marathon but she was probably just over-tired and over-caffeinated. "Clare still hasn't heard from Brian since that first voicemail. He may not know about Abby's note but he knows Clare's wired about this baby thing. He could have called," she said. "I guess we just have to sit tight until the next phone call. God, I hate that. Story of my life. Waiting for the phone to ring."

"Please – when did you ever have to wait for the phone to ring – apart from the book thing?"

"Don't call it a "thing", Tina said," – that's a pejorative term."

"Oh, you mean like "baby thing"?

"You're right. I'm a Bitch," she mouthed. "But you are too." Jane and Tina took their conversation to the office, away from customers and the ears of small children.

"I grant you," Jane said, "it's a weird situation. Brian may be off somewhere looking for Wonder Woman and

Abby may be having a hot weekend, but not together – whatever problems he and Clare may have been having."

Jane toyed with the idea of mentioning what Clare had told her in the kayak but decided against it. It wasn't Jane's secret to tell, and if Clare had wanted Tina to know about her indiscretion, she would have spilled the beans herself. Or announced it to the group over wine, as so many other announcements – good and bad – had been shared. Was a fling payback from Brian? *My infidelity cancels out your infidelity?*

"I've been going back and forth almost as much as you have," Jane said, "and I don't see Abby having an affair with *any* of our husbands. It's got to have been a joke."

"If she *didn't* run off with someone's husband," Tina said, "where the hell is she? Lying in a ditch somewhere?"

"Oh, please, not the ditch. I'm having flashbacks to my mother. There's traffic. They forgot. Something better came up. It's a million to one the person you're waiting for is actually *lying in a ditch*. That's just something people say because they don't want to instantly assume a friend or spouse is a thoughtless a-hole. Who invented that "lying in a ditch" line?"

"Some hack writer. I wish it had been me. It's good. Very visual. Look, you're not going to want to hear it, but, I do believe Abby is capable of it. She was always a little outside the group, wasn't she? One of us, but not really?"

It was a harsher assessment than Jane expected, unlike Tina's usual flip remarks. And it had the practiced sound of something Tina had said or thought before. Had something happened Jane didn't know about? Was that the way they felt about her, too? Was *she* a little outside the group? Like a resident who – no matter how long they lived someplace – would never be considered a "local" because they weren't born there. She waited for Tina to continue.

"I've been thinking," Tina said, "what if she *was* meeting someone? And then something went horribly wrong?"

"Like what?" Jane said.

"What if she really was planning to run off with someone's husband and one of them got cold feet. And the other one wasn't happy about it?"

"You're thinking like a mystery writer not a rational person. What are you saying? Do you know something you haven't told me?"

"Forget it," Tina said, "I should have kept my mouth shut." She clammed up and Jane regretted forcing the issue.

"Does Rachel know Abby's assistant called?"

Tina shook her head. "She's still at her mother's. Kate isn't back from upstate and Tomato Bob is – wherever the hell he is, eating beef jerky and pretending to be a mountain man. Why can't he just go to Vegas and get a lap dance, like most guys would if they had a weekend away from their wives?"

"Maybe she'd rather he eat beef jerky than some hooker in Vegas."

"Good point. Rachel doesn't know about this latest development. I didn't want to call her house this early and scare her mother, but I knew you'd be up anyway," she said, "makin' the donuts."

"Her mother's away, remember? And I don't do donuts. Has the assistant tried to call Abby's father?"

"Couldn't reach him either."

"There you go – they're still pretty close. Maybe Mac took her on a last minute trip. They're probably off somewhere having a blast."

When the Bitches were young they all had crushes on MacGregor Daniels. He was elegant, successful and rich.

What he did sounded so exotic compared to the other fathers. Jane's, in particular, who left one morning for a company softball game and never came home. His team lost.

"If she blew us off to go somewhere with daddy, she should have called instead of sending a fruit basket. And the note," Tina said. "What was that about if she's away with her father?" She had a point. "I think we should go back to Connecticut to be with Clare. She was pretty upset."

"So now we're *lobbying* for adulteress?"

"*I'm* lobbying for thoughtless wench with a hot date – preferably with someone we don't know," Tina said. "But I'm preparing for all the possibilities."

"I'm going to have to get back to you about Connecticut," Jane said. "I've been away for days and Mo and the others are running on fumes. And I've got twelve loaves of banana bread to bake. They're a special order and I can't take off again or Shanika will kill me. They're for her friend's shower."

"Banana bread? Your part-time Caribbean employee would be upset? You're the boss, for crissakes."

"That's why I have to be responsible. I have a business to run. I can't just leave. I'm the single one, remember? The orphan. No parents. No husband. No rich father."

"Let me get my violin. What about your partner, Glenn, *the good son*? Didn't he inherit any baking skills from his mama?"

"Are you kidding? The only dough he knows anything about is the kind you lose at the track. Oddly enough, he called before you broke in, but I think he was just getting home, not just getting up. He may have been drunk, talking about pina coladas on the dunes at six in the morning."

"You do have one regular and one spare!"

"Shut up. Neither of those guys is around and I have work to do. Bitch." This time the epithet was used as a term of endearment. To soften the harsh sound of Jane's earlier words. She had expected the mystery to be over by this time and instead it had ballooned. And truth be told, she was anxious to hear from Vincenzo. She rattled off a laundry list of reasons to not go back to Connecticut.

"Well, I'm going. I promised Clare. I'll call Rachel and she'll either come with me or go later with you. If her mom is out of town, I might as well go now. Got any muffins I can bring? I don't like to visit empty-handed."

"Can I give you day old?"

"Sure."

It killed Jane that her friend automatically assumed she would follow, even though she hadn't decided. She filled a bag with mini-muffins and a slab of poppyseed bread from the day before and told Tina she'd check in later.

Jane wasn't sure she *should* leave again. She couldn't expect part-timers to keep picking up the slack – especially since they'd worked extra shifts all weekend. That would cost her in overtime pay she couldn't afford. Besides, with the exception of the erratic Glenn Buonofiglio, who looked after a business better than an owner?

But she was a good Bitch and this was a group crisis so she scrolled through her saved numbers to see if someone – maybe one of her holiday helpers – could cover for her, in case she changed her mind.

CHAPTER 15

At first, Rachel Weiner thought it odd that her parents never re-purposed her bedroom after she and Bob married. Other parents turned their now-married children's rooms into home gyms or craft centers. Sharon Minsky's parents had turned hers into a meditation room – for two years anyway until Sharon filed for divorce and had to move back in. She's still sleeping on an inflatable bed and sharing closet space with a large stone Buddha. Now Rachel was glad her parents hadn't made any changes. Maybe they knew something that she didn't.

Gilda Weiner was nobody's fool. That's what people said about Rachel's mother ever since she was a young girl working part-time at her Grandma Dora's millinery shop in Philadelphia. Gilda was born there, right in the shop. Her mother was selling cotton duck to Bunny Schwarz when her water broke, so Gilda's first view of the world was the colorful mosaic of mercerized threads lining the walls of her grandmother's stockroom.

When Gilda was old enough to work after school she joined her mother and grandmother in the shop. Grandma

Dora didn't offer a salary, only a small commission on every bra, girdle and box of hosiery the granddaughter sold – a better deal anyway – and as a bonus she took the girl along on her monthly buying trips to Orchard Street in New York where they roamed the wholesale markets, treated themselves to eggplant sandwiches or bow ties and kasha at the Grand Dairy and filled shopping bags with merchandise for Dora's Strawberry Mansion storefront. On very productive days they bought rugelach for the long train ride home.

Dora's command of English, or lack of it, wasn't a problem in Philadelphia where most of her customers spoke Yiddish, but in New York, she was sometimes at a disadvantage with the younger wholesalers. Gilda's help was invaluable. More than once she prevented her grandmother from making a costly mistake due to miscommunication – intentional or otherwise. One time a vendor who didn't realize the women were together tried to substitute lesser quality merchandise for the brand Dora had chosen, explaining it away with a phrase she didn't understand. Gilda caught it and read the man the riot act. That was when she first earned the title "nobody's fool" and she wore it proudly.

Whenever Rachel and Bob visited Gilda, they stayed in her old bedroom and her father's office with its pullout sofa became Kate's room. It made the child feel grownup and sometimes her grandparents let her stay up well past her bedtime, filling her with Weiner family history, since none existed on her father's side. Tomato Bob was not their granddaughter's father.

Kate was conceived the summer after the Bitches' junior year in college. Jane and Rachel had stayed close to home in New York City – Brooklyn College and New York University. Tina and Clare had gone to schools upstate,

Syracuse and Vassar. Abby went to Georgetown – partly to be near her father, then based in Washington, D.C. Three years as hostess for her father had turned her into a woman while the other four were still girls, and that summer, it showed.

Tina was the only person who guessed. All Rachel had to do was throw up once on the way to the beach and her friend knew she was preggers. With three sons, Tina's mother had thought it best to get certain things out in the open early for her only daughter and Tina could spot someone who was knocked up a mile away.

Rachel had never mentioned Jason Berger to the others. They'd met on Memorial Day at the beach club where both were lifeguards. That early in the season there wasn't much action in the water but the young employees at the deserted concession stands and empty daycare center made up for it with parties and drinking contests that always ended with couples disappearing into the night.

After much talk, pleading, and reassurances, Rachel and the boy shared a sticky quickie in a cabana that hosted no further activity from them despite a repeat of the cajoling and flirting that had precipitated their initial encounter.

It was Rachel's first sexual experience and having crossed the Rubicon she wasn't sure what she was supposed to do next. Having said *yes* once, it seemed stupid to say *no* but she was afraid that daily doses of Dr. Berger's Magic Injection (his charming expression) would increase her chances of getting pregnant and/or getting a reputation, so she held him off.

She needn't have worried. By the Fourth of July he was besotted with another girl – Abby Daniels, just back from her junior year abroad. Rachel and Jason had lasted not quite sixty days – just long enough to have sex once, get pregnant and get dumped. Like the catchy pop tune from their youth it had been a cruel, cruel summer.

"Please don't tell me my mother was right," Tina had said, "once is enough?"

Pregnancy wasn't the only reason, but it proved a catalyst for Rachel transferring out of NYU. Changing schools was easier than having to explain a not-so immaculate conception. She'd also decided to become a vet and at the time the best school was in Pennsylvania.

When her condition could no longer be hidden she told her parents Kate's father was a foreign exchange student she'd met in State College. That way she could claim he went back to England and they wouldn't ask about him again. Strangely, Rachel didn't mind that much. It's not as if she'd fantasized riding off into the sunset with Jason – although it would have been nice to be asked. Her commitment was to the baby growing inside her.

Abby never knew who the father was. None of them did except for Tina. By Labor Day Abby had returned to Washington, and the boy was a mere footnote, one of many who'd tried desperately to get her attention and had done so only fleetingly before she moved on.

The first few years were tough for Rachel. Going to school while you're a single parent wasn't easy, but things got easier once the baby was born. There was no longer any need to hide the pregnancy or mumble lies about who and where the father was – abducted by aliens became her stock answer. If her parents didn't exactly believe the exchange student story, they never said. And at the end of the day, neither of his summer loves could have picked Jason Berger out of a one man lineup.

CHAPTER 16

Tina's cab pulled up in front of a large craftsman-style house in the old neighborhood where she and the others had played in backyards and obsessed over teachers and boys. Much of the borough had changed but small pockets still retained the neighborhood feel of the Brooklyn she remembered as a child – where on the first warm night of the year pizza palaces like Tortoni Gardens were packed with families dining al fresco in the glow of Murano glass sconces and the streets were lined with cars double and triple parked as people waited for tables or their to-go orders or just to see and be seen.

She looked at the suitcase in the backseat of the cab that she hadn't even had time to unpack. *There's still sand on it*, she thought, brushing it into the street. She'd need a new one if she was going on a book tour, if authors still did that. This one looked shabby, frayed around the seams. A made-in-China gift with purchase from Victoria's Secret.

And she'd have to stop clipping her own hair with cuticle scissors and get a real haircut. She might need a makeover for the book jacket picture – her publisher had asked for one. Twice.

The first time Abby had suggested Tina adopt a new look, she'd been offended. She'd cultivated her eclectic style early on when thrift-shopping was the only kind she could afford, and it was still her preferred mode of dressing. But she knew there was a thin line between eclectic and eccentric and she'd unintentionally crossed it a few times.

The upcoming book was making her self-centered. Or had she always been that way? For the last year she hadn't a thought in her head that didn't have to do with the book, the promotion or the wonderfulness and exploitation of – *her*. After this weekend she resolved to spend more time at home. Things could vanish so quickly – a home, a relationship, a life. She wouldn't have mentioned it to the others but, the bicycle accident and the incident in the kayak had made her realize life was a gift. Her marriage was a gift. But she and David had been working too hard. They'd become too focused on non-essentials.

When was the last time they'd taken an eighteen-hour vacation in a good hotel in the city? Just room service champagne and an enormous king-sized bed they wouldn't have to make in the morning? When was the last time she'd climbed into the sack in something more inspiring than a tank top and a pair of boxer shorts? Without her laptop or a legal pad in her hands? Very sexy indeed. She'd remedy that. If she had gotten nothing else out of The Weekend she'd gotten a wake-up call.

The Weiner house, which had seemed dark, creaky and old-fashioned when Tina was a child, was actually a lovely arts and crafts bungalow with a big covered porch, lots of oiled wood and three working fireplaces, one in Rachel's room where the five women had spent many sleepovers as children.

For some reason, she always remembered the tiles surrounding the fireplace – mottled shades of green which to youthful eyes had looked stained and mismatched but now appeared exquisitely suited to the character of the vintage home. She was glad Rachel's parents hadn't changed them, although she couldn't say why. Perhaps the surround was one of the few things from her past that remained intact.

Her own parents had moved to a larger, impersonal home on Long Island that held no old memories for Tina but would undoubtedly be etched in the brains of nieces and nephews who cannon-balled into their grandparents' pool and rode their bikes on the pristine sidewalks of the development which could have been anywhere in the U.S. with the possible exception of Brooklyn. Her brothers and their wives all lived nearby.

Tina entered Gilda's house, as everyone did, through a wooden gate that led to a small backyard, a detached garage and the side door to the kitchen. In all the years she'd visited she never come through the front door. In fact, the only time she'd seen it opened was the week they sat shiva for Lou Weiner, with distant cousins coming and going and neighbors bringing foil-wrapped dishes of food. There had also been a motley contingent that she learned were Lou Weiner's musician family. All shapes, sizes and colors. Tina remembered trying to cheer Rachel up by guessing which instrument they played by their looks – the skinny black guy must be the clarinet, the short, stocky man the drums, the twitchy guy, percussion.

Learning a lesson from her bakery entrance she rapped on the glass panel.

"Come on up, Tina. Door's open."

Tina climbed the narrow half-staircase to the kitchen. One look at the familiar wallpaper and she was transported to a time when the scent of hot chocolate with mini-marshmallows filled the air. The Weiner kitchen was the girls' before-and-after stop on fall and winter nights when they went ice skating in Prospect Park. Before, to apply make-up her own mother disapproved of, and after, to hold a post-mortem on the evening's crushes and flirtations.

In the summertime the Weiner kitchen was redolent with the smell of lemons and mint, which Rachel's mother chopped and floated in pitchers of sugary sweet concentrate and brought outside to the girls. They sat in the backyard baking themselves with sun reflectors and baby oil mixed with iodine or gloppy orange gel that made them look like professional wrestlers greased for competition. Was there really a time before everything made you fat, aged you or gave you cancer?

The two friends sat down at the table in Mrs. Weiner's breakfast nook. Rachel had been crying. Her face was puffy and her eyes were rubbed raw, making them look even greener against her fair skin. Could Rachel really believe Abby Daniels would chuck her thriving business, her friends and her glam lifestyle for Tomato Bob Price? His tomatoes weren't even that good.

Tina tried to lighten the mood with positive memories but stopped when she remembered most of them included Abby stories, all of which could have a different interpretation in light of recent events. She was dying to know if Tomato Bob had called but instead she cracked open the box from Sweet Dreams and fished out a muffin.

Tina saw the tears welling up again. She reached for the tissues – which had already seen plenty of action that morning – and handed the box to her friend. She shared what Abby's assistant had said about the cancelled appointments and what she feared it meant for Clare.

"Does Gilda still make that disgustingly sweet lemonade?"

"She does," Rachel said, through her sniffles. "I don't

know how she has any of her own teeth left but she does."

Rachel retrieved a blue Tupperware pitcher from the fridge and filled two glasses with the elixir of their youth. They each washed down two muffins.

"When that basket was delivered," Rachel said, "Brian was the first one I thought of. Vincenzo adores Jane. And David would be too frightened to leave you." Those last words escaped Rachel's mouth before she could stop them and once they did she winced at the tone.

"It's okay," Tina said, patting her friend's hand. "You couldn't help yourself. You're a bitch." Tina would not have put it the same way Rachel had, but she did think her marriage to David was solid. Of course they argued. All couples did. And she told herself it occurred less frequently than other couples she knew and about more trivial issues. Oddly enough, food and scheduling were at the top of that list. On all the major issues – money, sex, real estate, in-laws – they were in sync. (They were resoundingly *for* the first three and had some reservations about the fourth.) Compatibility. Likemindedness. They were the important things, weren't they? Still – what did she have to compare it to? Most couples didn't fight in public. They kept it in until they exploded at home. Or in the car. Lips tight. Nerves strained. Until they were someplace safe to unleash their shared fury, after which things settled down to a baseline.

She had never heard her parents say a cross word to each other. Frank and Donna Ruggiero could have been the warm, big-hearted Italian neighbors from a 1950's sitcom. Was that the gold standard for marital bliss? Or did her parents have their secrets too? She wanted to say *What about you?* but one of the great things about their friendship was not having to state the obvious.

Rachel splashed cold water on her face, patted dry with

a paper towel and checked the time on a noisy, yellowed wall clock that hung on the Weiner's kitchen wall for as long as either of them could remember. Different bird sounds for every hour. Nine o'clock was the most annoying, a shrieking, angry creature they'd happily never heard in real life.

"I can still see you," Rachel said, "standing on the counter one night, trying to change the time on that clock so my mother wouldn't realize how late we got in."

"It went haywire," Tina said, nodding. "All the backyard bird noises went off at the same time. It was as if a cat had broken into an aviary. I've never liked those clocks."

"Still works. She puts a piece of masking tape on the back with the date on it every time she replaces the batteries."

"Why?"

"I have no freaking idea," she said, shaking her head, laughing and wiping away tears.

The plan was for Tina and Rachel to go to Clare's, with Jane possibly meeting them in Connecticut later. Clare would put them up for the night as long as they didn't mind sleeping on sofas and Aero beds. They'd be there for her if she needed them, but until they left they polished off the day-old baked goods, drank lemonade and relived earth-shattering discussions and monumental decisions that had been made at that table. Whether or not to get matching tattoos. Long or short dresses for Spring Fling. Whether or not Tina should let Ryan Berkowitz get to second base. (No – they opted for matching pendant necklaces instead, floor-length, and definitely not.)

When it was time to leave Rachel excused herself and went to throw a few things in a bag. While Tina waited she called Sweet Dreams and Jane's cell and left messages on both numbers.

Rachel reappeared, freshly made up, her hair minus the scrungy. The black sneakers were exchanged for loafers and a blazer replaced the oversized sweater she'd lived in on the Cape.

"Jane's not answering,' Tina said. "She's ignoring me, but I've left voicemail. We should just go without her."

Rachel picked up her handbag and a tote and made a final house check – keys, lights, punch in security code for alarm, sixty seconds to leave.

"That's new," Tina said, letting herself be gently shoved out the door.

"I made Mom install it. The neighborhood's changing. It's not that it's unsafe, but there are so many new faces. Most of her friends have decamped to Florida to live in tidy white boxes but Gilda keeps saying *feet first,* as in that's how we'll have to carry her out. I guess I don't blame her."

"Like the song – *little boxes, little boxes . . . made of ticky tack.* My parents are, like, one step away from that. But they're close."

"Bob's parents are down there. I think that's the real reason she doesn't want to move to Florida. She'd have no excuse not to see them."

"Not everyone in Florida knows each other, do they?"

"Besides, she loves this house too much. I do, too," Rachel said. "It really feels like my home. And she works so hard on her garden. After forty years she says it's almost the way she wants it. She's out there from March through October moving bags of topsoil in a Radio Flyer cart that was old when I was a kid. We told her to get some help but she's so stubborn. She says they never do it right. Even watering. I didn't know you *could* water incorrectly."

Tina shrugged. "Gilda's a tough old bird. Where is she this early?"

"Today is casino day. Almost every day she has some event or excursion. She's more active in her community than I am."

"Does she think she'll get extra credits in heaven?"

"Don't laugh- I think she does! Once a month she takes the blue rinse crowd to the casinos for an overnight trip. On her way home she's picking up Kate," Rachel said, locking the door. "That'll be us in a few years. You're the take-*ers* and then before you know it, the take–*ees*."

"That's depressing. You'll have us wearing Depends by the time we get to Clare's. We're still young. Okay, not as young as that bimbo on the Cape."

"That's another thing," Rachel said. "Was she a bimbo or are we just getting older and less tolerant?"

"Anyone other than my husband who stands in my kitchen practically naked is a bimbo or a ho. *Dang it, girl, put on a cover-up.*"

"I guess you're right. Does David really stand in the kitchen naked?"

"Why, do you want to come over to watch?"

Rachel looked down and fumbled with her keys.

"Hey kiddo, I was joking. That was just me being me. Pay no attention. No one else does." If Tina had any doubts that Rachel and Tomato Bob were going through a rough patch, she didn't anymore. Had it been that long since Rachel had seen a naked man? That could make you cry. Tina opened the gate at the foot of the driveway and Rachel pointed a remote control opener at the garage door.

"This is new too," she said. "Last year Mom wrenched her back opening the old double door and she didn't tell us for weeks."

"Hey, my mother was afraid of the microwave for the first twenty years that she owned one."

"She's not intimidated by electronics – she knows more about the computer than I do. She just doesn't like to make changes to the house since my dad passed away."

Her reluctance to upgrade their home was not a sign that she was packing it in. If anything, Gilda had been even more active since her husband's funeral. She chaired AAUW meetings with her college friend Elaine Sattler and brought meals and companionship to homebound seniors, some of whom were not much older than she was. And she took seniors to Mohegan Sun for the early week specials which is where she was that morning, chaperoning two dozen septuagenarians on a trip to the Connecticut casino.

Rachel's dad, Lou, had been in advertising. For young girls that meant jingles and funny animation – too late for the martini and cigarette chic of the *Mad Men* era and painfully crude by today's glossy standards. Sometimes it was fun getting samples of products before they hit the shelves – shampoos and pimple creams – but Rachel's strongest memory of him was his love for music. When he wasn't making up ditties for clients he played jazz violin in bars and clubs and klezmer music at weddings and bar mitzvahs. Just for the love of it.

"Do you still have your father's old record collection?"

"I can't believe you remember that. Yeah. After I got married, Dad turned the basement into a music room. Funny, Abby once asked about the records, too."

"Didn't we all sneak into a wedding once where he was playing?" Tina asked.

"Wearing prom dresses so we would *blend.* Don't remind me. We got so busted for that one. Another of your harebrained ideas. Is it my imagination or were you constantly getting us into trouble?"

"We all contributed our fair share. Abby, too, but her plans always went off without a hitch. Remember the scheme to meet JFK Jr. by accosting him at a Knicks game and pretending to be reporters for some fictional newspaper?" It was unlikely he believed the girls but he'd been a good sport and when he died they were heartbroken and wept as if they'd really known him.

The women loaded their gear in the backseat of Rachel's car. Tina had the one cotton print duffel and Rachel a wheelie, the rubberized boat bag she'd taken for the weekend and a tote.

"How long are you planning to stay?" Tina asked.

"I don't know. Not long. I couldn't decide what to bring. I took a sleeping pill last night and I'm still fuzzy-headed. The Cape Cod bag probably would have been enough but I found myself packing another. Nerves, I guess. I haven't been thinking clearly this morning."

"You do seem distracted. Would you like me to drive?"

"I was hoping you'd offer. Thanks, Tina." She tossed her friend the keys, guided her as she backed out of the narrow driveway, then latched the wooden gate.

"It doesn't mean anything" Rachel said. "That note. There's probably a perfectly reasonable explanation for her missing our weekend."

Tina stared at the sky with the same impassive expression she wore when a student said something particularly dense and her position prevented her from saying *Are you stupid*?

"You're right. Abby's probably de-worming orphans in Uganda and just neglected to tell us."

"She could be."

"Rachel, we are gonna have to reevaluate your status as a Bitch. You are too good to be true."

CHAPTER 17

Rachel and Tina were quiet for the first half-hour of the journey. They'd talked so much already, what was left to say? On the way, they stopped at the same place they'd gone for iced coffees and a last pee break the previous week. The waitress remembered them. That's the sign of a good one, Tina thought. She must be the owner.

After five minutes on the road, Tina could see her friend was itching to say something.

"Okay. What?"

"The blender," Rachel said.

"The blender? Could you be more cryptic? What is that? A driving game you play with Kate? Am I supposed to name another appliance, like, the stackable washer/dryer?"

"This morning when you mentioned the lemonade. It was the *blender* that reminded me. Something stuck in my head," Rachel said.

"Probably all the sugar."

"This past June at Clare's pool party. You weren't there, you and David had a book thing."

Tina scrolled through the mental version of her

Microsoft Outlook calendar. "Oh yeah, symposium. I was supposed to be introduced to movers and shakers. Only person I met was this short, bald blogger who wanted to move and shake with me in the men's room."

"Uck!"

"Don't worry, I got the quote first. What does a blender have to do with anything?"

Brian had volunteered to pick up Abby from the train station and Rachel thought he'd been a little too eager. None of the others had noticed; Clare was busy coordinating the timing of the dishes as if choreographing the half-time show during the Super Bowl, and Rachel's husband, Bob, was trying to resuscitate a blender that expired mid-margarita.

"I'll go with you," Rachel had said.

"No, no, you stay with Clare. She may need another pair of hands. She may also need you to run out and buy a new blender." A gentle dig at Bob. The two men had never hit it off.

"He didn't *want* me to go, Tina. He wanted to be alone with Abby."

"He was being thoughtful," Tina said, not sure she believed her own words but what Jane said had registered and she gave Brian the benefit of the doubt. "I'm paraphrasing Jane and she may be right. If you start second-guessing every look and double-entendre of the last few years you'll drive yourself nuts."

"Maybe." Rachel let out a sigh and closed her eyes.

"You're not going to sleep again, are you? You must have gotten ten hours between yesterday's drive and last night. I read that's a sign of depression."

"I'm not depressed, I'm just neutral."

"This isn't neutral, and it's not like you. Is there more?"

Rachel kept quiet, but Tina could tell she still had something she wanted to say. Tina signaled a left, cut off a white Audi, and pulled into the far end of a Mobil station.

"Jeez," Rachel said. "Take it easy."

"Audi drivers are used to it. They cut people off all the time. Beemers too." She turned the engine off and stared at her friend. "We're not moving until you spit it out."

"We should probably drop this, but I can't help but feel that something's wrong," she said, shaking her head. "I know Brian said he was in London, but he could be anywhere. How would she know? It's not as if he's got a microchip implanted under his skin."

"I know they do that for dogs," Tina said. "Can you do that for husbands?"

"Listen, there was something more the day of the pool party. Brian downed two shots of vodka before leaving to pick up Abby. He looked excited and nervous to be going and I swear he checked himself out in the mirror three times before he left. As if it were a date."

"For pete's sake. Brian's always been vain. You primped and we're just driving to see Clare. And everybody flirts after a drink or two. Ninety-nine times out of a hundred they don't act on it. And even when they do, there's usually an embarrassed apology the next day and a vow to never speak of it again."

"Let me finish. It took them forty minutes longer to get back from the train station than that ride should have taken. Abby claimed her train hit something on the tracks and was delayed in the Bronx somewhere. She concocted this elaborate story about how the passengers had been evacuated and put on another train."

"What are you saying – they stopped for an afternoon delight on the way home? Where? There aren't exactly a lot of hot sheet motels in Clare's neck of the woods. You think they pulled into an empty MacMansion to do the deed?"

"I don't know where they went, but I do know there was no report of a mishap on Metro-North that day. I checked."

Tina saw her friend with new eyes and remembered that days earlier Rachel had been the one who'd called the florists on Cape Cod to find out about the fruit basket. "You *checked*? When exactly did you turn into Jessica Fletcher?"

Rachel let her head fall back on the headrest. She'd had an oft-ridiculed childhood addiction to *Murder She Wrote*. It was her weekly ritual with her parents and as a youngster she took great pride in guessing who the criminal was before Gilda and Lou did.

"Have you mentioned this to Clare?" Tina asked. Rachel shook her head. "Well, I don't think you should. Lots of people get picked up at the train station in Connecticut. We've picked Abby up there. Besides, despite his longtime obsession with Xena Warrior Princess, he loves Clare." She drummed her fingers on the steering wheel. "While you've been collecting evidence against Brian, I've been thinking about something else. Vincenzo and Jane aren't married. He's *her man*. The same phrasing in the note."

"You know," Rachel said, "I love that we've instantly taken our own husbands out of the running. Is it because we trust them or because we think they're not good enough for Abby?"

CHAPTER 18

The Didrikson home was in Winston Heights, a rural area with no sidewalks and not much vehicular traffic, so when a car was heard, it was not odd for an occupant to look out a window to see who it was, behavior that would seem neurotic in their old Brooklyn neighborhood. Tina saw the curtains flutter just as she turned into Clare's driveway. She reached over to gently rouse Rachel, who woke with a start and jerked up too fast against the seatbelt she'd forgotten she was wearing.

"Wake up, honey, we're here."

Disoriented, Rachel took a few minutes to unfasten her seatbelt, check herself in the mirror and collect her things. Clare opened the door before they'd had a chance to touch the bell. She looked haggard, as if she hadn't slept in days.

She let them in and they group-hugged in the entranceway. "I've been glued to the television," she said, a choke in her voice. "The police found a woman's body near the train station. They don't know who it is yet."

"Oh, no." Rachel and Tina dumped their things in the

entranceway and followed Clare to the family room where the local news station was tracking the story.

"Have they given a description?" Rachel said.

"Just that it's a woman in her thirties. No I.D. on the body." Adultery paled by comparison.

Rachel and Clare were stunned and near tears. Only Tina kept her head. "Look, I've already had the "lying in a ditch" conversation with Jane. The odds that this poor woman is Abby are a million to one."

"Oh, yeah. Jane texted. She's not coming."

"Great," Tina said. "We're in trouble if I'm expected to be the voice of reason."

"What about the fact that she still hasn't gotten in touch with anyone? We've been badmouthing her and she could be in the morgue." Rachel had been on a crying jag since before Tina had picked her up and the waterworks were about to start again.

"We need to go to the police," Clare said.

"Let's just think about that for a minute."

Clare stood up. "I'm making a fresh pot of coffee. Unless you want something stronger."

Tina shook her head. "Coffee's fine for now, but save the thought."

Clare went to the kitchen and returned with a tray of coffee and a plate of butter cookies that she set down on the large ottoman in front of the television.

"You look tired," Tina said.

"Why do people say that?" Clare said. "Was there ever a time when anyone answered *Thank you for acknowledging that I look like crap*?" Clare closed her eyes.

"Fine! I won't say anything else. I'll just sit here and watch the two of you blubbering over a total stranger." The strain of the last few days showed on all of them and Tina took it out on herself by snatching two sugar-coated cookies from the tray and wolfing them down.

"I do look like crap. I'm probably hung over. I had two glasses of scotch last night after you left."

"You partied without us?"

"It was hardly a party. I had another just before you got here. Hair of the dog."

The news report – and making a sizeable dent in Brian's bottle of twenty-year-old scotch – brought Clare to a very different conclusion than the others had reached. Tragic accident at the train station. Had to be Abby.

While anything was possible, it was also possible that Abby was with Elvis on their way to colonize the planet Zoran. Maybe Jane was right to have stayed away.

That morning, as soon as Clare saw the news report, she telephoned the local police who politely explained that a woman who didn't show up after saying she wouldn't was not considered a missing person. They wouldn't give her any specific information about the body unless she wanted to come down to the police station and make a report. Only if they thought there was even the slimmest chance the victim was known to her would they let her I.D. the body.

"I felt like an idiot," she said. "I came off like a hysterical female getting the vapors over nothing. Or one of those crazy people who try to inject themselves into a news story."

"Did you tell them *exactly* what the note said?"

"Hysterical *and* pathetic?" Clare said. "I was pacing myself until you guys came and we could go there together. In person. I simply said there was a message and we weren't sure we understood it."

"I don't believe it's Abby." Tina tried to sound confident, but what if something horrible had happened? Hadn't she even suggested that to Jane earlier? "It's ridiculous, but if you feel they blew you off and you want to talk to the cops again," Tina said, "we can all go. We can spread the crazy around so it's not just you."

"Tina, you really are a bitch." It was an exhausted, matter-of-fact statement Clare delivered without any trace of malice.

CHAPTER 19

The police station in Winston Heights was a white brick building just opposite the town library with its fluttering banner proclaiming its participation in One Book, One Town. It spoke well for the citizenry that the library's Costco-sized parking lot was ten times larger than the police station – perhaps they read more than they committed crimes.

A gray-haired woman at the front desk, civilian, addressed Clare by name. Either her call had been the morning joke or they didn't get many. She led the three women to a row of orange molded chairs outside the closed office door of Lieutenant John Patrick Crowley, the police officer who'd spoken earlier with Clare. Shadows on the frosted glass panel and sounds coming from within suggested the lieutenant was on the phone and either pacing or not alone.

"Please have a seat," she said. "I'll let . . . uh. . . the lieutenant know you're here." She almost slipped and called the younger man Jack or Pat, as she may have when no one else was there. But this was an official visit. She tapped on the door, opened it a crack and nodded, without saying a word.

"He'll be with you in two shakes. There's a vending machine in the back if you girls want something to drink, but it's best to use exact change. That machine steals quarters." She gave the women a motherly smile and scooted back to her post out front.

They waited in a thirty by ten hallway that held two round tables and about a dozen office chairs, most of them nested and stacked against a dirty wall. The opposite wall was home to stacks of boxes filled with papers and files, listing under their own weight. Thumb-tacked to the wall near the light switch hung a town planner calendar, this month featuring a local dry cleaner, who'd won a national spotting award.

"Am I hallucinating or was that Aunt Bea? And that would mean we're in Mayberry?" Tina whispered.

"Anything wrong with that?" Clare said. "There's a very low crime rate here. Lots of people would think that was a good thing. Rachel agrees me with me, don't you?"

"I'm all for law and order. I watch it all the time," Tina said. "I'm just wondering if they've actually solved any crimes before, other than Case of the Missing Quarters and the crime of who decorated this place."

Her words still hung in the air as the door opened.

"On occasion," Crowley said. He stood just over six feet, gray eyes, dark buzz cut hair with the jaw line and stance of a hero from a graphic novel. He held a clipboard in his folded arms and his shoulders nearly filled the doorframe. Tina wouldn't have been surprised if there had been a cape fluttering behind him. For once she was tongue-tied.

"As I already told Mrs. Didrikson, your friend is not missing by our definition of the word. There's isn't much we can do about someone who doesn't come to a party."

After only a few words Tina knew how Clare had felt

during her telephone conversation with the cop – hysterical and pathetic. Foolish. Even as the words came out it seemed clear their friend had either changed her mind about joining them or gotten a better offer. If it happened to be with one of their husbands it was unfortunate but hardly a police matter. Abby may have been horizontal somewhere, but on 400 thread count Egyptian cotton sheets, not in a ditch. Tina relayed what she knew and Crowley listened attentively, but didn't take notes.

"Sometimes people need to go off by themselves for a while. I'm not saying that's the case with your friend, but wouldn't you rather it be that than have her a victim of foul play."

"What about the woman you found?" Tina said.

"Identified. It looks like an accident, but that's all I can tell you. The victim was not Abby Daniels."

"Thank goodness. We're so relieved," Clare said, standing up. She hesitated. "But you did say I should get in touch if there were further developments. If we think there are any can we come back?"

"Of course. As you might expect, Mrs. Didrikson, this is a busy day." Crowley checked his watch. He humored them by taking down her description, but they had the feeling as soon as they left he and Aunt Bea and Floyd the barber would have a good laugh at their expense.

Just then a short, fireplug of a woman with a pixie haircut entered the hallway holding a cardboard tray with four coffees. "It's a jungle out there on double coupon day," she said. "Wait till you hear this – ." Officer Rosaria Guzman came in chattering about an altercation at the Stop and Shop parking lot that had escalated into fisticuffs when one pregnant woman made a sarcastic remark and another went off the rails. She rested the coffee on a file cabinet and stopped just short of finishing her story when she saw the women. "I'm sorry, lieutenant. I didn't realize anyone was with you. Betty's away from her desk."

Now it was Crowley's turn to feel foolish. *A catfight at the market between two bloodthirsty pregnant women? That'll get the investigative juices flowing.* "Quite all right, Officer Guzman. We're wrapping up here. Was there anything else, ladies?"

Tina stood and slung her handbag across her chest, with a satisfied smile. "Yes. Can you recommend a good place for donuts?"

CHAPTER 20

Winston Heights had no real downtown unless you counted the four-way stop where George Axelrod sold antiques and coffee until 3 p.m. which he and his wife thought was a civilized hour to stop work.

The firehouse might also have laid claim to the title of center of town. It stood opposite Firefighter Lucy's Café, a place Tina remembered well. She recalled each close encounter with a fireman ever since the Christmas she was eleven and her cousin Little Anthony (not to be confused with Little Tony) built a fire and neglected to open the fireplace flue. Within minutes, her aunt and uncle's home was filled with smoke and squealing children until four strapping men arrived to see what had set off the alarm and make sure the family Christmas tree was in no danger of going up in flames. It had made a lasting impression on Tina and all the Ruggieros, two of whom went on to join the department.

"Firefighter Lucy's is the closest place for coffee," Clare said, remembering her friend's fondness for broad-shouldered men in suspenders and tall rubber boots. "Although the food isn't the biggest attraction there."

"How far is it?" Tina asked.

"Five or ten minutes."

"Do you know the place that cop mentioned?"

Clare nodded. "Good desserts. Maybe twenty minutes from here but it's a nice drive – we can take the back roads."

They piled into Clare's vehicle and she pulled out of the police station lot. She turned left up a hill that took them past a middle school, a senior center and a grade school that looked like a high tech farm. She turned down a road roughly parallel to what locals thought of as the highway. "This is prettier and we can go almost as fast," she said.

As they drove, the properties got bigger, farther apart and harder to see from the road.

"Jeez, that one house is bigger than the strip mall where my office is," Rachel said. "Who lives there? Not really – but who can afford a house like that?"

"Beats me. I always think of them as hedge fund guys like my brother-in-law. They've got three-acre zoning here."

"Is that to keep the riff-raff out?"

"That's not the way the residents look at it. It preserves the open spaces."

"Like that one does?"

Clare slowed down to give the others a look at an infamous local landmark. If it had had any more white columns, banisters, cherubs and wrought iron lanterns it could have been in Disney World. "There's always the exception. That's the tacky house."

"Are you serious? Their name is Tacky?"

"No. Some kids used a Sharpie to write *tacky house on left* on the stop sign over there. They tried cleaning it off, but you can still see it. I feel for their neighbors."

The next home was gigantic. "Jeez, do these people *dress for dinner*? They look like they should have footmen," Tina said. Clare let her friends make the typical cracks and never let on that she spent close to an hour each morning trolling real estate websites and lusting over homes just like the ones they were making fun of.

Homes with enormous family rooms where children, relatives and extended family would gather for holidays and special occasions. Homes with kitchens and formal dining rooms with islands and tables laden with picture-perfect place settings and food they couldn't possibly finish. Clare knew it was her Norman Rockwell/Martha Stewart fantasy, and most real people had nothing remotely like that, but she didn't care, she wanted it. Or some version of it. The family compound.

Would she ever have that with Brian? Who couldn't commit to raising a child because he hadn't grown up himself? Would his extended family come dressed as characters from comic books – Elastic Girl? The Incredible Hulk? Sometimes she thought they'd have been better off if they hadn't patched things up after the affair.

For the rest of the drive the women weighed in on pools, gardens and the merits of plastic fences and decks over wooden ones and as Clare predicted, in twenty minutes they crunched onto a gravel lot where half a dozen SUVs similar to hers were parked in formation.

"Who says there's no diversity in the suburbs?" Tina said, getting out of the car. "Are you sure this isn't a dealership?" She was right. The only thing missing was the toothy, over-eager salesman jingling keys and offering to take them for a test drive.

The outdoor picnic tables were shaded by colorful umbrellas and crowded with three or four parties of women and children. The little ones ran between the tables and through a series of planters filled with a profusion of flowers while a multi-pierced teen with ink-black hair and fingernails to match served their mothers. She wore no headphones but moved her head rhythmically as if dancing to an inner iPod.

"Modern day suburbia," Clare said. "You've got your middle class women who don't work anymore – like me – and your scary-looking disaffected youth who do. That's diversity."

"Were we like that?" Tina asked. "So angry?"

"A lot of it's just fashion," Rachel said. "The same way it's hard to tell the real sluts from your basic mall rats. Some of the girls in Kate's class look like they're pushing thirty."

"This weekend made me feel old," Tina said. "It was supposed to have the opposite effect. What did we do wrong?"

"*We* did nothing," Rachel said. "C'mon, we'll share a plate of fried onion rings – that should make you feel like a teenager again."

"Only if they make me break out."

The women decided they'd have more privacy inside where they were greeted by a solitary waitress, hunched over her side of the counter, reading a paperback. She was almost as thin and goth as the teenager outside – perhaps they were mother and daughter. As they entered she straightened up and flashed a smile that seemed genuine.

"Greetings. Welcome to the Paradise Diner. The booth in the back is the A-list table, but it's yours for the taking. Most everyone else wants to be outside today. If there's a lull in the conversation that sightline has a good view of the ducks on the pond. There's half a dozen ducklings. They can be pretty entertaining." She was just friendly enough, but not pushy.

It wasn't likely the women would run out of things to talk about but they took her advice and slid into the booth as far away from the other patrons as possible. She brought them three glasses of water, placemats, set-ups and a stack of menus that she'd held tucked under one muscular arm that revealed a blue and green snake wrapped around the name Pete and covering the arm almost from shoulder to elbow.

"We're nutrition-agnostics here," she said. "We commingle the low-fat and high-fat offerings and trust that you'll be able to figure out which is the Jell-o and which is the chocolate cake without some cockamamie leaf or symbol next to the name. Choose your poison, but we're famous for our desserts." When the women nodded noncommittally, the waitress, sensing they were not there for her locally famous badinage, told them to take their time and holler when they were ready to order.

"She looks like she's been around," Tina said, surreptitiously trying to read the woman's other tats. "I always thought we should have gotten those ankle tattoos we talked about."

"I, for one, am glad that cooler heads prevailed. My ankles swelled up when I had Kate. That could have been ugly." It was Abby who vetoed the ink party and bought them the necklaces instead. Florentine gold chains with pendants in the shape of the letter B, which they all still had.

"She's always one step ahead of the rest of us," Rachel said.

The chat was light – shoes, hair, weight, the latest magic goo that claimed to take ten years off your face or ten pounds off your hips. Then they ordered – coffee and blueberry muffin for Clare, a turkey cranberry wrap for Rachel and a tuna melt with onion rings for Tina.

"You've been eating all day. How can you eat like that

and stay so slim?"

"Portion control . . . I won't eat it all."

Their food came and slowly the diet, real estate and shoe chat ground to a halt.

"Thank heavens it wasn't Abby they found," Rachel said.

Yes, thank heavens. But that begged the question – where the hell was she?

"I know she and Brian talked," Clare said, at last. "More than a few times. About his film project."

She cleared the condensation from her water glass one stripe at a time as she trailed off, muttering about how Abby and Brian had discussed a possible sponsorship from one of her high-end clients. Or as Abby had put it, *a symbiotic relationship*. Clare knew first-hand that work relationships could sometimes develop into more.

"Don't even think it," Rachel said. "Abby's our friend."

"Why?" Clare said. "Because twenty years ago we went to the same parties and made fun of the same people? Does that make for a lasting friendship?"

"That's not like you," Rachel said. "Wasn't she trying to help your husband? Wasn't she working on Tina's book publicity?"

"There's been a lot of talk, but I don't know that she's actually *done anything* on my behalf. That nitwit in her office didn't even seem to recognize me other than as one of Abby's friends."

"Publicity takes a lot of groundwork," Rachel said. "You can do a tremendous amount of work and not get any return."

"Is that supposed to make me feel better?"

"Let's stick to what we're talking about, okay? We came up here to help *Clare* feel better."

Their voices grew louder and this time they attracted the attention of another diner who'd arrived after they had.

Slightly younger than they were, she wore grubby painter's pants, frayed at the cuffs. Leather garden gloves stuck out of her back pocket. She and the waitress were locked in conversation the minute the newcomer ensconced herself at the counter. She gave only the slightest turn of her head, but it was enough to convince the women it was time to tone their conversation down or take it elsewhere.

CHAPTER 21

Later that night, Tina and Rachel were making themselves at home and Clare was entering from the garage with two bottles of wine when the phone rang.

"Clare," Tina yelled. "It's the phone. Shall I get it?"

By the time Clare reached the landline the call had gone into voicemail but she picked up once she caught the tail end of her husband's voicemail message.

"Oh, good, you're there," he said.

"Of course, I'm here, where else would I be? More to the point, where are you? Haven't you gotten my messages?"

He hadn't. He'd left so unexpectedly that he hadn't had time to upgrade his cell service.

"You couldn't borrow a phone? Where are you, in the Kalahari?"

Brian was just outside of London, staying with a friend of a friend because it was cheaper than a hotel.

"Jesus, Clare, did I miss the twenty-seventh baby update?" His comment stung. But she'd only make matters worse if she told him the real reason she'd been so anxious. Rachel pulled Tina into the kitchen to give Clare some privacy. On the way she plucked the wine bottles from the crook of her friend's arm.

"Are the others still with you?" Brian asked.

"Yes. Well, not Jane."

"Well, then all's right with the world." His voice had a too-familiar edge.

They exchanged how-are-yous as if they were strangers or slight acquaintances who didn't really want to know and would have been annoyed if actually told. Clare remembered to ask how his production meetings had gone, but Brian seemed reluctant to talk about them, perhaps knowing she didn't really care. It was too absurd to discuss comic books when so many more serious issues roiled in each of their minds.

"Are you coming home soon?" she asked.

"Of course. Unless those women have taken over my house and voted me off the island." They sighed in unison, one of the few times in months they'd been in sync.

When Clare and Brian were first married being apart was agony. Returning from business trips they couldn't wait the extra hour or two to be reunited and would pick each other up from the airport. Sometimes he'd tell her what to wear and they'd role play – he'd pretend to be the demanding boss or she'd be the expensive prostitute. Or vice versa. Once he pulled over to the far end of a rest stop and they made love in the back seat like teenagers. That someone might catch them in the act had made their encounter even more thrilling. She'd confided that to Rachel but her other friends would have been shocked if they knew how sexually adventurous Clare, the quiet Bitch, had been during those few heady months.

All that now seemed like something she'd read in a novel or woman's magazine or made up and resurrected to get through the mechanical, monthly ritual their physical relationship had turned into. Sex with Brian had become as exciting as a Pap smear. When had they stopped being crazy about each other? Was it something *she'd* done or not done, or was that simply the way it went after a few years of marriage – the slow inevitable transformation into brother and sister, or worse – two roommates who had little to say to each other apart from the logistics of food, transportation and control of the remote.

Brian gave Clare his flight information and estimated time of arrival and told her he'd take a cab or shuttle bus service from the airport. She saved the number of his borrowed phone just in case.

"It must be two in the morning where he is. What's he been doing? Here's Jane, considerate enough to get in touch all the way from exotic Brooklyn and my own husband can't be bothered to call when he's overseas."

"C'mon, Clare, you know it's a pain sometimes – with the time difference," Tina said. She tried to sound convincing but deep down she thought Brian was a dick for not calling.

"This is the twenty-first century," Clare said. "There's no real time difference anymore. He said he thought I'd called about *nothing*. Baby updates. I'm so glad he thinks they're *nothing*."

Tina read the pained expression on her friend's face and gave Clare's arm a squeeze. "At least you know he wasn't screwing around. That's good!" She was fulfilling her job as "the voice of reason" admirably.

"He'll be home tomorrow," Clare said, neither glad nor sorry, simply resigned to the fact that she and Brian would resume the off-kilter conversations and disagreeable, extended silences they'd been having for months as her trip to Kiev and the reality of the adoption got closer.

"I'm glad you two came back," she said. "I needed to hang on to that feeling that we're still together. The way we used to be."

"Let's get out of here," Tina said. "Movie, mall, meal – I don't care, just as long as it keeps us occupied and mostly out of the rain."

"We can't eat here. That old tin of cookies was the freshest thing in the pantry," Clare said. "I haven't gone food shopping since we got back from the Cape. Jeez, was that just yesterday?"

"Time flies when you're having fun."

"Fine. Food. That's a perfect excuse to go out. Maybe we'll bring back a movie, if any video stores are still left. Or we can buy a really awful direct-to-video movie at the drugstore.

Sometimes they're so bad they're better than the comedies. We'll have some laughs."

This time Tina insisted on Firefighter Lucy's. Rachel brought her things upstairs to the storage room/soon-to-be nursery and went to freshen up. Tina pulled out a makeup case, swiped some tinted balm on her lips and ran her fingers through her dark, wavy hair, massaging her scalp and fluffing her locks.

"Will we be passing the police station to get to Lucy's?" she asked. She shopped in Clare's coat closet for an umbrella or rain slicker and casually waited for an answer.

"Not unless you want to." Clare waited for an explanation. "You're doing that thing where you try to act nonchalant but have something on your mind. Do you *want* to stop at the police station?"

"I guess not. It's probably nothing, but I've been thinking . . . " The voice of reason was slipping away.

"You're right, then, it's probably nothing."

"Good, you're getting your sense of humor back, such as it is," Tina said. "It's just that I've been remembering the old days." She swung around to face the staircase, making sure Rachel wasn't around. "And thinking about Abby's note," she whispered. "*I've run off with one of your men.* Maybe she didn't mean one of our *husbands*."

Clare looked up, puzzled. "Not the sexy dentist theory again. My dentist is eighty years old and has hairy forearms. It may not be Brian but Abby has most definitely not run off with my dentist. Do you have someone in mind? Who's connected to us but isn't a husband? You think Jane knows why her father really left?"

"It's possible. Her mother might have said something. Deathbed confession?"

"Thanks, Mom."

Clare hoped her own mother would drop no bombshell revelations when she passed, not that there was any danger of that happening soon. Clare's mother had just celebrated her sixty-fifth birthday by climbing Mount Kilimanjaro with other members of her alumni association and made it known she had every intention of sticking around until Clare and Brian's child – however appropriated – got married and begat its own issue.

"A mother wouldn't do that," Clare said, shaking her head, "not unless she was *Mommie Dearest.* Jane's mom was nice – y'know, before."

"I'm not saying she was Joan Crawford, but it can't have been easy keeping a secret like that buried all these years. Who knows? Maybe it wasn't even intentional." Tina said. "She was on a lot of medication toward the end. What if it leaked out accidentally in some drug-induced stupor?"

"And then what? Jane waited five years to confront Abby? You are way too imaginative. Wouldn't she have told us?"

"Do you really think we know everything there is to know about each other?" Tina said. "We've all got secrets."

That was true enough. There were things Clare hadn't shared with the group. Her affair with the intern, for one. Clare handed her friend a lightweight barn jacket, took out a similar one that must have been Brian's and put it on. She tucked her hair under the corduroy collar, then looked for three wide-brimmed hats to protect them from the rain on the sprint from door to car.

"It's a possibility. Think about it," Tina said, putting on the borrowed jacket. "She's not here with the rest of us. She's been the least concerned about Abby's note. Maybe that's because she knows where Abby is. Or maybe . . . " she leaned in to whisper "Charles Monaghan has come back to try his luck again."

"Shush, Rachel's coming. I don't think she knows." She raised her voice. "Rachel, do you need a jacket?"

She shook her head. "No, I'm fine," she said, bouncing down the stairs. "I've got a hoodie. You don't think I know what?"

CHAPTER 22

Older man, younger girl. The story was older than dirt and just as boring. Unless it happened to someone you knew. An absentee mother and a father who worked long hours and traveled extensively for business. A worldly young woman used to the attentions of men. It was a perfect storm of circumstances that had happened countless times before and it happened about six months after Abby and her father moved to Brooklyn.

Mac Daniels had inherited a small publishing company from a maiden aunt. The aunt, after whom Abby was named, had self-published a series of spiral-bound books – helpful hints, home remedies and recipes she'd collected over the years – and sold the booklets, first to her church group and then, encouraged by their popularity, door to door.

When Mac graduated from college he worked with her, selling and later re-packaging them until professional enough to offer to the nation's largest catalog companies – Lillian Vernon, Reader's Digest and Publisher's Central Bureau – where they turned into surprise bestsellers.

His genius, and a surprise rave review from Martha

Stewart, turned the *Ask Abby* books into a cottage industry. By the time the aunt died Mac was fielding offers from major publishing houses and when he finally sold it was worth millions.

Newfound wealth got Daniels seats on a number of boards and, ultimately, something he hadn't given much thought to while building his publishing empire – a wife. He was pushing forty and so far all the women he'd met in his adult life had either been employees or customers. When he met Maria Orsini, he was charmed, tired of being alone and ready to commit.

After they married, Daniels was offered the executive vice-presidency of a private philanthropic foundation started by the man who'd bought his aunt's company. Accompanied by his new wife and, shortly after, their infant daughter, Mac Daniels traveled the world deciding which worthy groups should be the recipients of his employer's largesse.

When they moved to Brooklyn, Abby's father was spearheading a new foundation to aid natural disaster victims. She was alone quite a bit before they hired a live-in housekeeper, Mrs. Dedham.

"I remember her," Rachel said. "She was creepy. Like the evil matron at some turn-of-the-century girl's school."

The girls might not have liked her but she was a stabilizing force in the Daniels household. And in the absence of a mother, Abby had sometimes confided in her. Things she couldn't or wouldn't share with contemporaries. Sensibly Mrs. Dedham shared her charge's observations with the girl's father.

An older man had developed an inappropriate attraction to Abby. Mac Daniels had been forced to intervene. He confronted the man privately and, unbeknownst to Abby, had gotten a restraining order to keep the man away.

"How long did the affair last?" Rachel asked.

"It wasn't an affair," Clare said. "Nothing physical ever transpired between Abby and Charles Monaghan."

"Holy shit," Rachel said. "Jane's father? Does she know?"

"She knew something happened. Most people assumed Monaghan left his wife because he fell in love with another woman. They just didn't know she was sixteen."

"Ick. Where was I? Did I totally have my head up my butt that year?"

"Pretty much," Tina said, not unkindly. "I think it was advanced placement year. And you and your mother were deciding which of your two hundred extra-curricular activities you would list in the yearbook."

"Not fair," Clare said. "We were kids. And it was the eighties. Certain subjects were still taboo back then. Or if not taboo, no one broadcast them. People weren't subjected to the full range of horrific news anyone with a computer and online connection can get nowadays. I shudder to think what the level of discourse is going to be by the time the baby gets old enough for her own computer."

"Don't worry," Tina said. "We'll probably all have chips implanted in our brains by then. We'll all know instantly any time a celebrity cuts her hair or breaks up with someone."

"That's a load off my mind." Clare distributed bucket hats. "C'mon, let's get out of here. It's pouring. Pick a hat."

"I'm not wearing that," Tina said. "It has the name of a superhero on it. I'll look like an idiot."

"Take the freaking hat."

CHAPTER 23

Sweet Dreams was less sweet when Vincenzo wasn't there. Mo and Shanika had been great hires – honest, responsible, fun and always up for extra hours – but they weren't Vincenzo. He was the only one Jane could complain to or express doubts or worries to. With everyone else she had to be positive and upbeat, whether she felt it or not.

The staff was small. All she could afford except for holiday help she brought on in December and June, two months when everyone was celebrating something and no one was on a diet. Mo Heedles had moved from Massachusetts and was putting herself through Brooklyn Law School at night, and Shanika Callwood was an artist and single mother. Her boyfriend was a reggae musician who occasionally brought his guitar to the bakery to serenade her and anyone else who happened to be there. The first time he did it was the couple's one-month anniversary.

"My Andy is a romantic boy," she'd say with a mischievous smile. Other anniversaries followed. First kiss. First whatever. Eventually, Jane and Andy made the performances official and now he played every Thursday night for tips and desserts that he took home for his roommates.

The atmosphere at Sweet Dreams was collegial but as the boss Jane had to enforce certain boundaries, although whenever she did she was uncomfortable. When Vincenzo was working it felt like a party. One big Italian family, with mama in the kitchen making dinner. His instructions were requests. Mo and Shanika were relatives and the customers their guests. But not that day. Vincenzo still hadn't checked in and Jane was damned if she was going to chase him down like some needy teenager.

At midday, the front door sprang open and in breezed Glenn Buonofiglio, bracketed by two of his innumerable cousins. His companions always seemed to be cousins but that didn't surprise Jane since any older men she'd ever seen him with were referred to as "uncles."

"How are my three favorite cupcakes," he boomed. "Vanilla, chocolate and strawberry? Am I right?" He stood with his arms out wide as if waiting for the three women to rush to him for an embrace. None of them did.

Shanika dipped her chin in disapproval but said nothing. She didn't have to; Jane knew what she was thinking – *ass-hole*. Mo blushed and hooked her straight blond hair behind one ear in a move that made the rest of her stick-straight hair drape charmingly to one side.

It seemed impossible for Glenn and his compatriots to engage in any conversation with a woman that wasn't flirtatious. Offensive even, if you were the type who took offense. But Jane had gotten used to it with Tina's brothers when they were younger. She assumed a certain type of Italian male from Brooklyn did it and then grew out of it, but not Glenn and his posse of cugines who seemed to revel in their retro behavior.

"Hey, partner," Jane said. "Contact from you twice in

one day. Has hell officially frozen over and I just haven't checked my emails?"

He wagged a playful finger at her. "You, you, you."

Two cousins busied themselves at the counter trading gambits that Jane suspected never went anywhere, although Mo seemed interested in the thickset one she'd heard Glenn call Johnny Boy.

"Can we talk?" he said, suddenly serious. He lowered his voice. "Not here."

Jane led Glenn into the backroom. *Not another marriage proposal*, she thought. Over the phone it was a joke, a harmless pattern they'd fallen into. In person, it would be flat-out weird. Would he get on his knees? Would there be a ring?

"This is nice," he said. "I like what you've done with the place. The posters, the sofa . . ." He moved his hands in a well-known gesture for having sex that made Jane inwardly groan but she kept smiling.

"So Glenn, how's your girlfriend?"

"What girlfriend? You mean Roseanne? I told you we're childhood friends. She's had a crush on me for years. Can you blame her? We're more like . . . buddies, you know."

It was sweet – and strangely delicate of him to leave out the offending adjective which would more accurately describe their relationship.

"That's not what she says."

"You know her. She's a crazy kid."

Jane did know about Roseanne. She knew that his temporary, non-girlfriend Roseanne Sicigniano had been his "buddy" off and on for eight years, had an older brother nicknamed The Chin and had suggested to Jane the first time they'd met that she'd have the brother perform some anesthetic-free cosmetic surgery on Jane if she ever heard that Glenn was stepping out on her with the skinny Irish chick. Because Roseanne and Glenn were secretly engaged. So secretly even Glenn didn't seem to know.

At a loss for words when the bride-to-be and two of her henchmen-like ladies-in-waiting delivered this announcement, Jane regrouped quickly, congratulating the woman, offering to make the wedding cake and trying to find comfort in the fact that Roseanne thought she was skinny.

"I don't know," Glenn said, "I haven't seen her for a while. Fuggageddaboud her. This is serious business."

If he'd said he wanted to talk about the films of Lina Wertmuller or the disappearing ice shelf Jane couldn't have been more surprised. Previous business conversations with Glenn had revolved around the midnight delivery of the aforementioned espresso maker and the discovery of a source for cupcake decorations in the shape of a cornicello, the curved Italian horn that kept away malocchio, the evil eye.

She inspected Glenn's face for signs that he was joking. Were he and Ann-Marie unhappy with their investment? Did he want to pull out of the business now that his construction company was taking off? It wouldn't take an MBA to tell Jane she couldn't afford to buy them out if that was where the conversation was leading. But she was getting ahead of herself.

"Sit down," she said. "Do you want some coffee? Shanika made elephant ears."

"No, no. I'm good." Not a positive sign. Glenn was a good eater. If he didn't want free food this must be serious. Just then she regretted not being on her way to Clare's. She wished she was anyplace else and able to postpone this conversation. Jane closed the door to give them some privacy.

"What's on your mind, partner?"

CHAPTER 24

Jane left work early. Minutes after she got home she dove head first into a one-inch thick sandwich of Skippy super chunk peanut butter and Smucker's red raspberry jam. Funny really, considering her baking skills, but PB&J could be ready in an instant. You didn't need to measure anything and there were no pots or bowls to clean.

Peanut butter and jelly or jam had been Jane's comfort food for as long as she could remember. When her mother wasn't baking Food Channel-worthy desserts she didn't much think about food. Tuna salad and mac and cheese became Jane's go-to dinners after her father left and the two females were on their own, but nothing said "quick fix" to Jane like PB&J. This time she washed it down with a small bottle of Moet, something she allowed herself when she was home and reasonably certain she'd be alone or alone with Vincenzo.

She popped the last bite in her mouth and considered wolfing down another when she heard the key in the lock. She stiffened. Only one other person had the key, but the last few days had been so weird she was no longer sure of anything . . .

"Cara, did you miss me?" Vincenzo Palmieri dropped his bag and rushed to kiss her.

"How is Renzo?" Jane asked coolly, not moving.

"I don't know. Fine, I suppose. Why are you asking about him?"

"Weren't you in Italy?"

"Would I go to Italy without you? I was in California. To see Marco."

Had Mo gotten the message wrong and mixed up the brothers? Had Jane misinterpreted? She shook off his questions and the slight buzz she'd gotten from the alcohol. There were no checked baggage tags on his suitcase which would indicate which airport he'd flown into and out of, but the bag was small enough so that he might have gone carryon. Or he might have torn them off. She hated that she even looked.

"So, what's up with Marco?"

"Nothing you need to worry about. I sat next to a dreadful woman on the flight home and had to pretend to be asleep even though I wanted to watch the Jennifer Aniston movie – you know how she reminds me of my beautiful girl. Aren't you happy to see me? Is Buonofiglio back there, hiding in the closet? Where is he? I will a-fight him to the death."

It was a silly private joke. A line from a scratchy black and white film they'd watched together – Fred Astaire and Ginger Rogers and a bunch of actors who didn't even pretend to be convincing with their frankly fake Italian accents.

She hadn't realized she was shaking until he wrapped his arms around her. Her arms stayed at her sides with her hands behind her back.

"Are you angry with me?" Vincenzo's hands slid down from her shoulders to the small of her back where he found the jar of peanut butter she still gripped. He pulled back but still held her shoulders. "Cara mia, I go away for a few days and you're hitting the hard stuff? Tell me what it is."

Over the years she'd gotten used to the longish hair, perennial five o'clock shadow and the full lips, but she was always won over anew by the dark, crinkly eyes that drew her in almost as palpably as his arms did. She had fallen in lust with him in that skinny t-shirt, but the deal was sealed when she saw him hand a cupcake to a three-year-old girl, scraping off the icing and redoing it until it met the child's exacting specifications. That was the way he was looking at her now. He was the kindest man she'd ever been in a relationship with. How could she have doubted his affections? Even briefly.

"Why didn't you call?" she asked.

"I was giving you space," Vincenzo said. "I knew you'd have spent the whole weekend with those *stregas*. Am I wrong?"

"They're not witches. They're bitches. There's a difference. Well, there's some overlap."

Vincenzo liked her friends well enough, but Abby was the only one he'd ever felt close to. Perhaps because she knew Marco, and spoke to Vincenzo in Italian. It sometimes chafed that he and Abby shared exchanges and confidences closed to her, but why shouldn't they? Wasn't it a good thing her friends liked him? Wasn't that the reason many friends drifted apart – because they didn't like your man, or vice versa?

She put the peanut butter on the table and pulled him over to the sofa. "I've had a very bizarre weekend. And today is Monday and it hasn't gotten better. Abby didn't show up at the Cape and it sent the others into a tizzy."

"Ah, they need her more than you do," he said.

"What do you mean?"

"They need her to make them feel special. You don't."

"It was a little more than that. Then this afternoon Glenn waltzes in and starts blathering on about families and children and now that his construction business is doing well he wants to settle down. I couldn't tell if he was proposing again or telling me he wanted out of Sweet Dreams. Ten minutes into his speech he got flustered and stormed out. I still don't know what he was talking about. I don't know if I have a stalker for a partner or my business is in trouble. And you weren't here. That's why I hit the peanut butter."

"I'm here now. Let me make it better, cara." He stroked her face.

Jane was aware her breath was still faintly peanut-y and she'd been in the same clothes since five a.m. but Vincenzo didn't seem to mind. He lifted the edges of her lightweight sweater and pulled it over her head, tousling her hair. Underneath she was wearing one of his t-shirts.

"You look better in my guinea tee than I do," he said, draping her sweater over the arm of the sofa. "Do you always wear my clothes when I'm not here?"

"Sometimes."

"But not the bottoms, I hope."

"You'll have to check for yourself."

They tossed the extra pillows on the floor and made love on the sofa. It wasn't the reunion she'd envisioned but he was there and he loved her and that was all that mattered. Not the artificial trappings of candlelight, silky camisoles or even clean teeth, just Vincenzo slowly unzipping her jeans and stopping to kiss her every inch of the way.

CHAPTER 25

Firefighter Lucy had been called that ever since she charged fearlessly into the Baldacci family's smoke and flame-filled kitchen and helped them escape the consequences of an unattended risotto. Lucy was anointed a hero and made an honorary fireman at a ceremony over which the mayor of Winston Heights had presided. Once the celebration died down, she missed the adrenaline rush so she joined the department as a volunteer.

Half of her restaurant was a screened porch where customers froze their butts off in the winter unless huddled near one of the space heaters. The other half was a renovated barn with one long counter where orders were placed and waitresses brought meals to a collection of mismatched chairs and tables scattered about under a ceiling festooned with t-shirts, banners and patches from firehouses all over the northeast. Maybe all over the world. On weekends a line of diners wrapped around the building waiting to get in.

Rachel, Clare and Tina shook off the rain and left their umbrellas and dripping jackets near the book swap rack at the restaurant's entrance, then made a beeline for a table in the middle of the screened room to avoid the sideways rain. A small group of firemen on the far side of the room facing the firehouse – either off-duty or not yet on – nodded appreciatively as the trio came in. Tina returned the favor.

"Brian doesn't like this place," Clare said, settling in. "I only come here without him."

"Can you blame him?" Tina said. "Self-preservation. The same instinct keeps me out of bars and restaurants in New York that cater to twenty-somethings and model-types. Why would I go there? So I can feel like a hag?" She smiled at the firemen, imagining them still in their heavy pants and suspenders but without the annoying t-shirts. She made a mental note to write firemen into her next book so she could justify research trips to firehouses.

"David and I are considering a move to the 'burbs," she said to the others. "Well, I am anyway. Forgive me, but the bar is just a tad lower here. I could have another ten years of *cute* before it turns into the dreaded *she must have been attractive in her day.* After my book comes out and it's a boffo success maybe we'll buy an old Victorian house in Madison or Guilford. I stayed at an inn in that area once – over a restaurant. It was like something out of an old movie – the pub with rooms to let upstairs. So quaint."

"And the smell of beer and smoke wafting up into the guest rooms? Charming." Clare said. "Those quaint houses are always better to stay in for a night or two than they are to own. Everything is off-plumb. It's like being on a ship – crooked tables, crooked pictures. And they're like foreign cars – something always goes wrong, the parts are hard to find, and nothing is ever standard. Rent, don't buy."

Tina imagined Clare and Brian having the foreign car discussion and Clare launching into a diatribe like the one she'd just delivered. She was right, of course, but Tina would have liked the fantasy to last longer. Her friend was a little too good at reality. It was one of the reasons Tina didn't enjoy talking to Clare about the novel. Clare wouldn't intentionally be negative or unsupportive but she was likely to recite depressing statistics about falling book sales and bookstore closings and how weight-loss books, thinly veiled soft-core porn, and celebrity bios were the only genres selling nowadays, not even realizing she was taking the wind out of Tina's sails.

Abby was always better at listening to dreams than Clare was. You could tell her you were trying out for the Yankees or planning to swim the English Channel and she would listen intently, and then say – seriously – that she knew someone who knew someone who might be able to help. And she did know many someones. Maybe it was all publicist's B.S. but at least she didn't burst your bubble in the name of practicality and common sense, two things Tina felt were highly overrated. She wondered if Brian felt the same way about Clare sometimes. Particularly with regards to that same tired project he'd been shopping for years.

"Seven or eight acres, at least." Tina continued, undeterred. "So I can have a nice big garden like my grandmother. Get a couple of goats so we don't have to mow the lawn. Some fig trees. Masses of basil. Maybe Bob can teach me how to grow tomatoes."

Rachel laughed uncomfortably. "Yes," she said, "I can just see the two of you starting a seed exchange."

"You've killed silk flowers," Clare said.

"They were fake eucalyptus branches and how did I know you weren't supposed to water them? Maybe grapes," she added, visualizing herself in a large picture hat and elbow length garden gloves. "We can make our own wine – get listed on the Connecticut Wine Trail. What should we call our vintage? My first thought was Bitch's Brew but that has too many other connotations. And wine isn't really a brew is it?"

That was Tina. Telling stories. Spinning tales.

Only Abby had read her book in its entirety. Not even David. The others had seen excerpts, carefully chosen for their eyes only. Tina had defended that decision by rationalizing that if they hated it she'd be crushed and if they'd said they loved it she wouldn't believe them, so why bother? Besides, other writers had told her that friends inevitably saw much of themselves in all the good characters and none of their own failings in any of the bad ones. That could cause problems since she had – consciously or not – bestowed some of their mannerisms and speech patterns on a few of her characters. The Bitches could dissect it, and her, after it was stacked high at their local bookstores.

They ordered three bowls of Lucy's Famous Four Alarm Chili and two glasses of red wine. Clare was driving so she chose iced coffee. Before the chili came they were treated to another round by the firemen, and that revived Tina's discussion of local real estate and her fictional vineyard, which the women played at naming.

After two glasses of wine Rachel had the courage to bring up the subject of Charles Monaghan. "You don't *really* think he's back, do you?"

"I don't know," Tina said. "In some ways it's easier to believe it's the bogey-man from our youth than to think it's one of our husbands."

None of the three women had thought about Charles Monaghan for decades. Charles Monaghan was tall and slim, an endodorph like Jane, and he'd met Jane's mom at the University of North Carolina where he'd gotten a basketball scholarship and she'd been a straight A student from nearby Apex. An early injury meant Charles spent more time on the bench than on the hardwood and he became fascinated by the sport's endless range of statistics. That was how he got into his field, demographics and list management, the antediluvian precursor to the sophisticated algorithms and targeted marketing done today.

Rachel, Clare and Tina had all thought Jane's dad was dreamy until MacGregor Daniels entered their lives. Charles' Ken-doll looks suddenly seemed generic compared to Daniels' striking appearance, cosmopolitan manners and casual references to places and things far beyond Brooklyn and "the city." Charles was white bread; Mac Daniels was french toast.

At recitals, sports events and school plays parents were welcomed, tolerated and eventually discouraged (as the girls got older) and if anyone had noticed Jane's father around more once Abby joined their circle it wasn't mentioned until after he disappeared.

Traditionally it was the mothers who showed up for daytime events, except for Abby's – still in Italy – and Jane's, a southerner who felt strange and out of place in Brooklyn. When Charles Monaghan started making his appearance all the women applauded his interest in his daughter's extra-curricular activities, particularly since their own husbands left heel marks in their driveways from being dragged to events – unless their daughters had a solo or were likely to score the winning shot. Some of the mothers even began primping, swapping the Mom Jeans for hipper clothing and styling their hair instead of scooping it, 80's-style, into a claw-like clip.

"Remember Helen Fleckstein's mom with the curly perm and *Flashdance* outfit? I would have been mortified,"

Rachel said. "She practically screamed *do me now!*"

In one day things changed. Maybe it was a congratulatory hug between Charles Monaghan and Abby Daniels that lasted a beat too long. A jock-like pat on the butt that lingered. Or maybe it was a flicker of desire in his eyes that could no longer be disguised as team spirit. And they finally noticed that Jane's mom was never there.

No one said anything out loud, but like a herd of gazelles that snaps their heads up when lions are nearby the mothers were all at once aware that something wasn't right with Charles Monaghan. His presence became suspect. After games the girls were hustled into cars that no longer had room for Monaghan or they were taken for celebratory meals in the opposite direction from where they knew Charles eventually had to be.

Then Clare and Tina heard their mothers speaking in hushed tones about something shameful that had happened or was in danger of happening. To their young ears shameful meant only one thing – sex.

Sex was the great mystery of their youth. Snippets of information were pooled, compared, and dissected on long walks and at sleepovers, aided by literature and videos pilfered from the Ruggiero brothers' extensive archives. Although the girls were aching to know what had transpired they were never brave enough to ask Abby or heartless enough to ask Jane so the Incident, as it became known in the two girls' minds, grew until it faded, replaced by fresher, juicier incidents for which they had more salacious details.

"I can't believe you never said anything to me," Rachel said, in shock that her two of her best friends had kept this secret from her.

"You didn't seem to know," Clare said.

"And what if it wasn't true," Tina added. "It's not as if we were 100% sure."

"That didn't stop you from saying all those horrible things about Helen Fleckstein's mother."

"That was different. Helen wasn't one of us."

After Monaghan disappeared, Jane and Abby grew closer. Perhaps it was the shared misfortune of coming from a single parent home but some of the mothers believed it was a unmentionable experience which somehow bound them together.

Rachel nursed her wine, ignored her chili. She no longer knew which of her memories to trust. In retrospect, her mother *had* shown a degree of wariness whenever Abby came to visit, but over-the-top affection and warmth whenever Jane was there.

"I wonder if my mother knew."

"I don't think any of our mothers would have wanted to scare us," Clare said. "Mine might have warned me to be careful, but only in that general *keep your knees together and don't ride in cars with strange boys* way."

"My parents were a split decision," Tina said, draining her glass. "My mother was convinced Abby and Jane's father did the deed and my dad thought it was all wishful thinking on Charles Monaghan's part."

"You *talked* about it with your *parents*?" Clare was stunned. The full extent of her own birds-and-bees conversation was the embarrassed and embarrassing presentation of a box of tampons, which her mother had rushed through accompanied by a fortifying double martini (for the mother, not the daughter). As a teen Clare was as likely to discuss sex with her parents as to announce she was dropping out of high school to join the circus.

"Of course not," Tina said. "I eavesdropped. My

bedroom was in between my parents and my brothers. I could hear everything – that's how I learned about life. That and my brothers' magazine collection." She looked around to make sure the waitress wasn't within earshot and that action had the opposite effect, unconsciously calling the woman to their table.

"You need something, honey? I'll be right there." The waitress hustled over, anxious to please.

"No, no, we're good. Thank you," Tina said.

"Are you finished with these?" she asked.

"Yes to the chili. No to the drinks," Tina said. The woman collected dishes and paper placemats, clearing the table quickly.

"Dessert? We've got peach pie, cherry, apple and a caramel flan."

"Apple pie with a scoop of vanilla," Tina said. The waitress was pleased. The bigger the check, the bigger the tip.

"You eat like a twelve-year-old boy," Rachel said. "It's beyond annoying."

The waitress returned and set down Tina's order on a fresh placemat. She brought three forks. "Just in case," she said, before leaving.

"Should we mention this to the police?" Clare said, after the waitress left.

"That we've found a good place for apple pie? Feel free."

"Stop being a wise guy. Charles Monaghan."

"You want to talk to them a third time? And tell them what? Something may or not have happened twenty years ago between a man you haven't seen in decades and the woman they don't think is missing? Let me know how that works out. I'll stay here, get another slice of pie and make nice to the firemen."

"You know, it's odd," Rachel said. "I thought about the

wording of Abby's card too –*I've run off with one of your men* – but it didn't lead me to Jane's *father*." She searched her friends' faces for confirmation. "Well, it's true. Jane and Vincenzo *aren't* officially husband and wife. He's her *man*. I mean – would it even be adultery?"

"It would be worse," Tina said. "Despicable. Lifetime Movie Channel motive for murder." She pushed the pie and placemat into the center of the table. We have to stop talking about this. We could simply call her – or would that be too retro?"

"I am not calling Abby to ask her if she's screwing my husband," Clare said. "Or anybody's husband. It's too ridiculous and you're right, we should stop talking about it."

Clare shifted the placemat, picked up a fork and took a small bite. She stared at the table. "But I am curious to know where she is."

"Fine. Tomorrow morning after we leave, Rachel and I will go to her office. Just for a casual visit to an old, dear friend."

CHAPTER 26

The Abigail Daniels Agency was twelve years old, founded not long after Abby left the publishing house where she'd gotten her start. She'd hit it off with one of their best-selling authors and the man jumped at the chance to hire Abby as his personal publicist. There were no hard feelings from her former employer; they effectively still had her services and she'd helped the author launch a book series, DVDs, a magazine and a cable television show. And the rumors of her affair with the man were no longer their concern.

Abby was demanding, brusque, and on occasion so sarcastic that an intern or two had retreated to the restroom until the pink tinge faded from around his eyes. But she was never intentionally mean, and if you emerged unscathed from her Bitches version of Navy Seals training you were rewarded by learning a lot about publicity. And you had fun doing it as long as you didn't expect a lot of "way-to-gos" and "attaboys." A slight smile and a "well done" was high praise from Abby.

Tina found parking on West 23rd Street around the corner from Abby's building, an ochre-colored warehouse sandwiched in between a livery company and a Salvation Army donation center. The sidewalk was lined with food trucks ready to make the afternoon diaspora into the city and offering every ethnic food from chollos to falafels.

The two women barely fit in the building's elevator. It rattled and shook and threatened to plummet to the basement, lurching past each floor before they were ejected onto the sixteenth which was marked with signs and arrows for photography studios, edit suites and small production companies.

The newest worker bee at the Daniels Agency was Chip Kellerman. Shockingly thin with no shoulders or hips to speak of, he had spiky, bleached hair, Buddy Holly glasses and a complexion so pale Tina wouldn't have been surprised to find a coffin and a handful of earth from his homeland stashed in his cubicle. All in black with a form-fitting vest over his chicken chest, he was wringing his hands like Uriah Heap when Tina and Rachel emerged from the elevator. Rachel thought she saw the guy suck down a pill but it might have been an Altoid. He flashed them a fake, two-second smile and punched a code into the security system leading his visitors through heavy glass doors into the loft-like space.

The room was about six thousand square feet of open floor plan – exposed pipes and unadorned windows. The concrete floor was painted and the few actual walls held mixed media installations and original art. It was hip and minimalist, like the agency's founder.

Eight employees in similar funereal garb lifted their heads, determined that the women were "no one" and kept murmuring into their headsets and furiously clicking on their keyboards.

"We can talk in Ms. Daniels' office," Kellerman said,

looking around. "I don't think we need to disturb everyone else."

The women followed him into a spacious office with smoked glass privacy windows on one wall and an expansive view of the Hudson opposite it. The furnishings were an eclectic mix of high and low style dominated by an enormous, mirrored armoire. Kellerman shut the door.

"Is there an official dress code here?" Rachel asked.

"What? Oh, it's just easier to wear black in case we have to go to a meeting or event on short notice. Dress it up or dress it down. Abby keeps a closet full of accessories in case anyone needs to borrow something at the last minute. Besides, she believes it contributes to the company's harmony. And, well. . . she's the boss. Please sit down."

Kellerman seemed to consider occupying Abby's high-backed leather chair, but couldn't bring himself to do it, as if She Who Must Be Obeyed might suddenly sweep in and dress him down for it. He pulled three black wire chairs into a semi-circle in front of the desk. Only he and Rachel sat. Tina strolled around the room, taking in the view from all sides.

She drifted to a bookcase filled with framed certificates and awards, and lingered over a photograph of Abby, the former mayor's arm draped around her shoulder. Good grief. Would Abby really have time to give Tina's novel the push it needed or would she be too busy hanging out with hizzoner and hand her baby over to Nosferatu here?

"There's a larger staff than the last time I visited," she said.

"We've grown," Kellerman said. "We have travel and leisure, consumer products and home furnishings, publishing and media, beauty and fashion, food and wine." He ticked off the categories as if reading from the company's promotional literature or pitching a prospective client.

"Abby is very well-connected."

Talk about stating the obvious. They just wanted to know who she'd been well-connected to the past weekend. Kellerman was in full-blown P.R. mode and they let him continue talking on the outside chance that he'd say something interesting. Which he did.

"Rumors are flying," he said, "that we're about to be acquired."

"By whom?"

"That's the beauty of rumors – it doesn't really matter. It's one of the reasons the staff out there is so busy. People want to make sure they're considered indispensible and none of their projects is falling through the cracks."

They were probably dusting off their resumes, too, if the rumors were true. No matter how *kumbaya* the press releases, mergers or acquisitions were always followed by bloodlettings. Tina wondered if she could get one of the other publicists cheap if Abby really was selling her company and running off with Clare's or Jane's man.

"I'm a bitch," she said, under her breath.

"Excuse me?"

"I have an itch," she said, quickly, scratching an imaginary bite on her arm. It was a good thing Kellerman was looking at her and not Rachel or he'd have seen the incredulous look appear on her face.

"If it's true and the company is about to be acquired, I say hats off. Abby's amazing," he said. "I can't say she isn't tough but everyone in that outside office would chain themselves to their desks overnight if Abby said they needed to. Two or three times in the past year we did – not the chains, but stayed overnight – just to meet a deadline. And each time, Abby closed the office the next day and took us all to Bliss for a spa day. She knows how to treat people.

Once you've proven yourself." He said it with pride, letting the women know that he'd survived Abby's trial by fire.

"You don't need to tell us. She's one of our dearest friends. That's why we were so disappointed not to see her. We happened to be in the neighborhood and thought we'd drop by to see if she'd come into the office or checked in with you since the message you left for Clare. Has she?"

When he was toeing the party line in pre-packaged sound bites he was fine, but asked a straight question for which he hadn't rehearsed an answer, Kellerman froze. He fished in his vest pocket and took out a small white pill, not an Altoid, and sucked it down. "Allergies." He shook his head so hard Tina thought she could hear marbles rattling.

"When was the last time you saw her?" she asked.

"Let's see." He frowned and touched his forehead as if communing with the spirits. "It was last Thursday morning. I got here at around 8 a.m. and she was just leaving. She was supposed to go to her meetings – one in Greenwich and the other in New Canaan – then hook up with you. I didn't know the details of that part – when or where – just that she wouldn't be in the office on Friday. I was surprised to learn she'd cancelled her meetings."

Six days a week Abby Daniels had a standing 5:00 a.m. workout date with a former Syracuse linebacker. She routinely went to her office straight from the gym to check in with overseas contacts, including a high-end eyeglass manufacturer in Italy. That account, referred by her mother had marked the beginning of a cautious rapprochement between the two of them.

"Sometimes, early in the morning I catch snippets of her conversation in Italian. I've never met her mom, only her father. She's seems very fond of her mother."

"Does she?"

As far as Tina and Rachel knew there was still a lot of distance between Abby and her mother but they didn't dispute what he said for fear that he'd clam up. But Kellerman saw a look pass between them and worried that he'd taken a misstep. That they'd tell Abby he'd been gossiping about her.

His own face grew paler. He rushed through a list of generic statements and compliments to counter what might have been a faux pas. *Of course, I don't anything about her private life. She's a genius. Everyone loves her. She has more style than anyone I've ever met. She can wear a Hanes boys' t-shirt and make it look like couture.*

"That certainly is a talent," Tina said, deadpan. The crack sailed right over the assistant's head. Were all her employees like that? Of course they were. Insincerity was the local currency in the publicity world. That's what they did for a living. Everything was fabulous until the next thing that was fabulous. Hopefully they'd be telling people *she* was fabulous soon.

"Doesn't Abby have a second in command? I remember meeting someone else here when my book deal was announced last year." She paused, waiting for the light to dawn in Kellerman's eyes but it didn't come. "He took a lot of information from me for the press release. Which, by the way, I haven't seen yet."

"A year ago that would have been Evan Wyatt but he resigned and no one has moved into his position yet, so I guess I'm number two – unofficially, since I'm the office manager and executive assistant. That's unofficial, of course. Not for publication."

Good lord, Tina thought, what a worrier. Who cared what it said on this guy's business card? But did that mean no one had replaced the guy who'd been working on *her* book? Tina was never good at hiding irritation, disdain or rage and she was experiencing the nascent symptoms of all three.

Kellerman pressed two fingers on either side of his forehead, silently praying Tina wouldn't ask for details about her own book which he'd been meaning to read but hadn't.

He got a reprieve when they heard a timid rap on the glass door. He jumped up, glad to be away from Tina's next question. One of the other employees, an Asian girl with a severe China doll haircut and lips so red and exaggerated they might have been made of wax, handed him a large glossy shopping bag. He muttered something about using petty cash for a tip.

"I don't have the key," the girl said, *you idiot* hanging in the air.

"Oh, right. Just a sec, Lisa." Kellerman put down the bag. "I'll be right back." He fished a key ring from the right hand pocket of his vest and excused himself. He left the bag in Abby's office.

"What's that?" Rachel asked, trying to peek inside the bag.

"A purchase from La Perla," Tina said. "That must have set someone back a nice chunk of change."

"What's La Perla?" Rachel said.

"High-end nightie shop," Tina said, using one finger to move the tissue paper and peek inside the bag without tearing the raised, gold seal. "Jeez, Rachel you're starting to scare me. I suddenly have the vision of you and Bob walking around in grown-up Doctor Dentons and it isn't pretty. I know, I know – you don't need to say it. I'm a bitch."

Kellerman returned quickly and Tina pretended to be admiring a signed photo of Abby and The Famous Author.

"I guess she won't need this now," he said, unlocking the armoire and slipping the bag underneath a rack of black clothing.

"Why not?" Tina asked. "Is there an expiration date on it?"

Chip Kellerman laughed uneasily. "No, Abby expected it to arrive last week. She was disappointed because she wanted to take it with her."

Tina wouldn't have thought frothy lingerie was anything one would need for an all-girls weekend on Cape Cod. But it might be something to pack if you expected another kind of engagement – either before or instead of their all-girls' reunion. She mentally kicked herself for not thinking to look for a gift card in the bag.

It took some finessing but the women learned it wasn't unusual for Abby Daniels to receive deliveries of new, insanely expensive lingerie. Especially in the last two to three months.

"Who was she supposed to be meeting in Connecticut?" Tina asked. She tried to sound casual and if Rachel hadn't known what her friend was getting it she would have thought nothing of the question. But Kellerman didn't read her question as personal interest. He saw corporate espionage. He hesitated, twisting a ring on one of his bony fingers.

"Was there anything different about this trip?" Tina asked.

"What do you mean?"

"Did she suggest she wouldn't be here Monday morning? Tell you to throw the yogurt out of the fridge? Remind you to water the plants?"

Kellerman shook his head. "We have a plant service that comes in every week." He was either dynamically stupid or intentionally obtuse.

"No matter," Tina said. "We understand. Professional discretion. She'll explain it all when we see her. As I said, we were just in the neighborhood."

Kellerman was getting antsy but didn't want to be rude to the boss' friends, particularly one who was a client – even a non-paying one. Tina commented on photos in the office and mentioned her book a second time to make the man feel guilty and buy them time in case she thought of anything else to ask him.

Then Tina's eyes fell on a slip of paper wedged under a candy dish on Abby's desk. A car service receipt. To Rachel's surprise Tina reached for and unwrapped a butterscotch candy from the bowl. She casually popped it in her mouth.

"We should be going," she slurped. "We just took a chance we might catch her."

Kellerman looked relieved and stood up to show them out when suddenly, Tina started coughing. Slowly at first, then more violently.

"Water. Ack! Get me some water!" She pounded on her chest and Rachel, alarmed, got up to do the same on her friend's back. "Something's stuck . . . "

Kellerman ran out of Abby's office. As soon as he did, Tina plucked the piece of paper from Abby's desk and shoved it in her jeans pocket. "What are you doing?" Rachel whispered, still pounding away.

"Go easy on the back," Tina whispered, "I like my teeth. This is what's known as creating a diversion."

Kellerman returned holding two bottles of water.

"Flat or fizzy?"

CHAPTER 27

"Flat or fizzy? Can you believe that guy? I'm choking – or pretending to – and he's asking what kind of designer water I want? A different world, my friend."

Tina glanced at the pilfered scrap of paper as they waited for Rachel's car in the West Side parking lot and tried to make sense of it. Kellerman said Abby Daniels left her office Thursday at 8:00 in the morning. The Black Diamond Car Service was supposed to pick her up and take her to Connecticut.

"Is there a destination address?" Rachel asked.

"It just says CPG, Greenwich. Sounds like a power company. Do they use P.R. firms?"

"Every time they screw something up. Could it be a company name? Maybe someone's initials?" Nothing leapt to mind, but they could Google the initials on a smart-phone on the way back to Brooklyn.

Once their car came, Tina took the wheel again and navigated in and out of the New York streets like a newly arrived immigrant cab driver. She got them to the West Side Highway in record time.

"I'm impressed," Rachel said. "I'm embarrassed to admit this, but I can't parallel park anymore. I've forgotten how. That's like forgetting your native tongue."

"I'm not surprised. You have got to spend more time in the city."

Rachel knew where this line of conversation was heading. It had started with the Dr. Dentons comment. She should have nipped it in the bud then. She didn't want to hear that she was quarantined in the Pennsylvania suburbs with a man who wasn't worthy of her. But the truth was, she thought the same thing herself a few times a week. It just wasn't safe for her to hear it from outside sources. Especially one whose opinion she'd respected since the age of eight.

She made a conscious effort to talk about lighter subjects than broken marriages and philandering husbands. That left Rachel's daughter Kate and Tina's book. Rachel knew that childless women – even good friends – had a threshold of about six minutes when it came to hearing about someone's kid, besides, she was lost in her own thoughts so she let Tina ramble on about her book, a humorous mystery set in a private school, planned as the first in a series. For most of the drive she chattered about electronic rights and guest blogs and things that mattered as little to her as school districts and advanced placement courses mattered to Tina.

Despite the optimistic chat, Tina was nervous. It was exciting to be soon-to-be-published, like being engaged. With presents delivered every day. Then you got married and the day went too fast. The gifts stopped coming. You were no longer a fiancée or a bride, just a boring married lady. Was that what it would be like once her book came out? After this thing that she'd wanted for so long finally happened – then what?

She wondered if that was what it was like to have a child. Nine months of anticipation and people fawning over you and then a couple of years of non-stop poop and pee. Mountains of stinky diapers. And an inability to utter a sentence that didn't have a moronic, singsong rhythm to it. *Yes you are my little sweet potato!*

Tina admired Rachel for having done it – and mostly on her own until Tomato Bob came along. And now Clare, who was moving heaven and earth to acquire a child no matter how far she had to go or how much it might cost. She wasn't sure she and David were ready.

CHAPTER 28

"Best two hundred and fifty dollars I ever spent," the woman said, flattening out the placemat. "Who says advertising doesn't work? Where'd you get this – Firefighter Lucy's? That girl's better than the *New York Times* classifieds."

The ad had read *Think the rat is cheating? Call Nina Mazzo. Reasonable rates. Discretion guaranteed. Free consultation.* Clare had seen it peeking out from under Tina's slab of apple pie the night before, alongside ads for handymen, personalized mugs and computer geek services. She had shoved the paper placemat in her pocket when she went back to the table to leave a tip.

Clare's GPS system had led her through a maze of warehouses and manufacturing companies near the railroad station to a small office sandwiched between a ceramic tile showroom and a beauty supply distributor. The location did seem incongruous but what did she know? The only private investigators she'd heard of were Sam Spade, Sherlock Holmes and Magnum, P.I., but all she could remember about their offices was that Holmes kept his opium in a slipper. Not helpful under the circumstances.

Nina's office was filled with an abundance of oversized furniture, suggesting either a perception problem or a recent downsizing from larger quarters. Neither inspired confidence but having made the drive Clare thought it couldn't hurt to ask a few questions.

Mazzo was a middle-aged, rangy, blonde with short, spiky hair showing a thick stripe of intentional black roots. The ad said her specialty was tracking down cheating husbands and deadbeat dads, a mission she pursued as relentlessly as Inspector Javert, because, she told Clare, as a former cop in Bridgeport she'd seen first-hand the wrecked lives they left in their wake.

"Why did you leave the force?" Clare asked.

"I got tired of seeing the victims. You see that too often and it starts to feel like television. Not real. This way I choose my clients as much as they choose me."

Mazzo's livelihood depended on other people's bad behavior and there was no shortage of bad behavior in the suburbs as she discovered in the eight years since she'd hung out her shingle.

"I had a slow patch when the market was down," Mazzo admitted. She caught herself just before saying she was grateful the lull had ended because business – and infidelity, deception and criminal behavior – had picked up.

Clare explained why she was there. Partly.

"Abby is a publicist with her own agency. Her assistant was surprised that she cancelled those meetings. Apparently they had taken some time to set up. The assistant didn't even know until the clients called to reschedule."

Mazzo nodded gravely and took notes on a fresh legal pad. "So she was supposed to meet you and your friends, you got a note, but, you think she might have come to some harm. Is that it? Have you notified the police?"

Clare nodded. "The most positive thing I can say about our experience with a member of local law enforcement is that he had the decency to stifle his laughter. He told us it wasn't a missing persons matter. This man Crowley seemed more interested in a catfight at the local supermarket." She ratcheted down, not wanting to sound ridiculous and overreacting.

So far, Clare hadn't mentioned the details in the note. But why shouldn't she? She could walk out of this office and never see the woman again, who cared if some woman in a cramped office thought she and her friends were fools? When she told Mazzo the exact wording of the note instead of being less interested – like the police had been – Mazzo's eyes lit up.

"Now we're talking," the detective said.

So much juicier than her most recent case – divorced man kidnapping ex-wife's dog and driving to Canada with it. That had taken two weeks and involved customs issues. And the dog really liked the ex-husband better. The ex-wife had only pursued her canine rights to torture the man, so Mazzo had found it tough to return the dog to a woman who'd probably just stick the pooch in a kennel. Divorces could get ugly.

This cast, though, had promise – no kids, no dogs. And from the sound of it, a bunch of upstanding citizens who would be easy to trace. She calculated how much she might earn on a short-term job and what she might buy. She did need a new printer.

"In all likelihood," Clare said, "this will sort itself out in a day or two but frankly it's been on our minds – and your ad did say Free Consultation."

Nina Mazzo capped her pen. She'd meant to change the wording in that ad, but the print shop had cranked out

100,000 placemats – that's why the per unit cost had been so cheap. Unless she could convince Firefighter Lucy to shred them she was doomed to giving free advice to dozens, if not hundreds of anxious wives and desperate parents until the placemats were reprinted.

"Crowley's a good man," she said, seeing the money she imagined disappearing from her bank account along with the new printer. "He's right. It's not against the law to change plans," Nina said, studying Clare's face. Was she really worried for her friend's safety or was she trying to track down an errant husband? There was no reason to trample anyone's feelings but time was money so she laid it on the line.

"What if your friend doesn't want to be found?"

"She runs her own business," Clare said. "She's not going to just disappear of her own volition."

She gave Mazzo only as many details about the various players and relationships as the investigator needed. Mazzo gave her the rundown on what she might accomplish in two days, the shortest gig she would take. She told Clare she was licensed in New York and Connecticut and could send operatives to either location.

"You can do that?" Clare said.

"It's my job. I also have reciprocal arrangements with P.I.s in other states, if it looks like that might be necessary. Look, I have to ask – what if I find her and she *is* holed up in some love shack with one of your men?"

CHAPTER 29

When Tina's parents moved, the three-bedroom rent-controlled apartment she grew up in was hers for the taking, and the cardinal rule of New York real estate was that you never gave up a rent-controlled apartment. Landlords resorted to all manner of trickery to remove rent-controlled tenants so when such a lease was in the family it was passed down like an heirloom. That's where she and Rachel were when Tina made the call.

"Was it really necessary to fake an Asian accent?"

"Never hurts to keep your hand in. I might go back to acting one day," Tina said.

"Before or after you win the Pulitzer for fiction?" Rachel said. "Do you think she believed you? I think the accent faded the longer you talked."

"Does it matter? She told us what we wanted to know. The most recent trips were to CPG Industries."

"What or who is that?"

"Shorthand for a society decorator who doesn't want people to know she's using a publicist. Almost all the other Connecticut drop-offs were to a marina, but they stopped about six months ago."

"Wasn't that when she broke up with that investment banker?"

"Bingo. He had a boat he kept in the Long Island Sound. Stamford, I think. So all those trips to Connecticut were not to see Brian Didrikson on the sly. I'm so glad the billing clerk at the car service was chatty. Evelyn. She may go in the next book.

"Anyway, Evelyn said Abby never got picked up that morning. At least not by the Black Diamond Car Service. Someone called the night before and cancelled the reservation."

"Didn't Kellerman say he *saw* her get picked up?"

"He saw a black car come and she got in. He assumed it was Black Diamond. Why wouldn't he? All those cars look the same."

They were deep in gossip mode when Tina's mobile rang.

"David!"

After a few minutes, Rachel excused herself and let Tina gush, coo and sweet talk in private. She didn't want to start resenting her friend for having a happy marriage.

"It's going well at the writers' conference," Tina said, when she returned. "They love him! Abby's agency handles publicity for the conference. She recommended David for the gig when the other guy got sick. Bless Abby for getting him this chance."

"That would be the same Abby we've been suspicious of for days?"

"I know – I know what you've been thinking, but it can't be true. Maybe it was your own insecurities that made you doubt her."

"What *I've* been thinking?," Rachel said. "It's what we've all been thinking at various times. You question your relationship. You're wracked with self-doubt. You wonder if you're doing the right thing for your child by staying. You wonder if it'll hurt more if you stay or if you go. I wish I was you, Tina. You've got no problems. No responsibilities. No kid. No single aging parent to look after and worry about. A guy you still like to look at naked. And a new chapter in your life. What have I got?"

Well, it wasn't the fear of losing Tomato Bob that had been troubling Rachel. It was the fear of keeping him.

"You know what you've got. A wonderful daughter. A mother who'd walk through fire for you. And good friends who love you. You saved my life. You're responsible for me now."

"I didn't save your life, it was that couple who gave you CPR, not me. Besides, I've never understood that saying. Shouldn't you be responsible for me now?"

"If that's the case. I'm responsible. It's decided. Wherever Abby is, she's not with one of our husbands."

CHAPTER 30

"Jane, I need your help."

She and Vincenzo were in bed when Mac Daniels called and it took a while for his voice to register. She straightened up and pulled her robe together as if somehow he could see her.

"What is it?" she asked. "Is Abby okay?"

"That's just it – I don't know."

It wasn't Chip Kellerman's message that had worried Abby's father. Every time the Daniels Agency went after a new account, Abby threw herself into the pursuit. And she didn't always reveal it to the underlings until she was close to sealing the deal. But it was unusual for her not to share her work with her father, to get his advice. She'd been a little more secretive lately. Mac had chalked it up to a client he might not approve of. Or a new romance.

He wasn't concerned at all until the manager from Abby's building called. Someone on Abby's floor thought they smelled a gas leak. And none of the neighbors had seen Abby for days.

"I can count on one hand the number of times we

haven't spoken on a Sunday night. It's our little ritual. When we spoke last week, she said she had a surprise for me. That was the last I heard from her."

"I can remember your Sunday night dinners when we were kids," Jane said. "They were very special to her. I was quite jealous," she added, just to make him laugh. But they were both worried.

"You were always my favorite, Janie. Abby's too, although I suppose I shouldn't say that."

Mac knew Jane had the security code to Abby's apartment from the time the Daniels were traveling and had a painting shipped home. Jane went to the apartment to sign for it. Now he wanted her to go to Abby's to make sure she was all right.

"Will you do it, Janie? It's probably nothing, but you'll help an old man sleep better tonight."

"Of course, Mr. Daniels. Vincenzo and I weren't doing anything." Vincenzo looked hurt and slid his fingers up her thigh to her bikini line. Jane slapped Vincenzo's hand away.

"We'll call you later, but as you say, I'm sure everything is all right. Good-bye."

"What are you doing? I was on the phone."

"It's exciting to have to keep still when you don't want to, isn't it?"

"We have to get dressed."

"Why?"

"Mac hasn't heard from Abby and he's asked me to look in on her."

"I think that assistant of Abby's has made you all nervous for no good reason. What's his name . . . Evan? He's a drama queen."

"That was the old one. The new one's named Chip," Jane said. "Complete deer in the headlights, but he'd cut off an arm for Abby. Why haven't I ever had an assistant who anticipated my every need? Not only do these boys make her schedule, they know when to hold her calls, bring her tea and change the water in the floral arrangements. They probably give her foot massages, too."

"Lover?" Vincenzo asked, taking Jane's feet and putting them in his lap.

"Not likely. This is hero worship."

"Abby's a grown woman," he said, "and she'll get in touch when she wants to. Why are you all fussing so much?" He started rubbing, slow lazy circles on the bottoms of her feet.

"Is that all I had to do? Mention something once and you'll do it? How is it we've been together for so long and I just learned this?"

Vincenzo shrugged. "I can't deny, it helps if the request is made right after really good sex."

"Well, it wasn't the assistant who made Mac nervous. Get dressed, I'll tell you on the way." She looked for her panties and bra in the tangled sheets.

"It's true, you know. Other girls were jealous of her popularity. I was jealous of Abby because of her father," Jane said, getting dressed. "God knows mine was nobody's idea of Bill Cosby so compared to him Abby's was a knight in shining armor. After my dad left, Mac Daniels was very kind to me. I even fantasized Abby's father and my mother might get together," she said, pulling on her pants.

"Not really – it was just a childish dream. Kid stuff. I don't even know if he ever officially divorced his wife."

"Italian divorces take forever," Vincenzo said. "And they can be unpleasant. Why are you all so worried?"

How much would she tell him? Every last silly detail from The Weekend? Her own fleeting doubts? It was too hard to decide so she told him everything.

"You do realize that your friends are all insane? And when you are together they infect you with their lunacy?" He was joking, but there was a shred of truth to what he said. Without Abby there, had they simply spun their own relationship issues into a ridiculous and unlikely scenario?

"You think Abby is with the tomato man?" Vincenzo said. "The comic book boy? Abby Daniels is a consort for a king."

Jane was glad he liked her friend but that was not the way she expected him to put it.

"Cara, please tell me you didn't think it was me."

"Of course not."

As tired as he was from the cross country flight, Vincenzo agreed to go with her after a quick shower and a change of clothes.

"We can go to Chinatown or Little Italy after we leave Abby's. Some place close," Jane said, hoping to make the outing fun instead of a bizarre chore.

"Good. Man does not live by peanut butter alone."

"I'm a little worried about entering her apartment unannounced."

"So announce yourself. Call before you leave. Call from her lobby. If she's there, she'll answer. I don't see Abby cowering in the closet in her own apartment."

It killed her that he was so practical. "What is with you and hiding in the closet?"

"Isn't that what they do in the American movies . . . the romantic comedies? That's how we foreigners learn our first words in English – from movies and old tv shows. I learned English from Erik Estrada."

Within fifteen minutes they were in the bakery's mini-van, Vincenzo at the wheel, turning onto the Manhattan Bridge.

"I never doubted you," Jane said.

"I know, *cara*."

He patted her hand and headed for Abby's apartment – without needing to be reminded of her address.

CHAPTER 31

Miles apart, in Connecticut and Arizona, two men who could not have been more different returned from recent journeys. One reeked, having spent four days in 105-degree weather in an un-air-conditioned car. To improve his gas mileage and reduce his carbon footprint. The other carried the faint woodsy scent of the three single malt scotches he'd consumed on his trans-Atlantic flight home.

After being virtually incommunicado for days, Bob Price checked his cell phone messages and found the same three, all from Rachel. She was still in Brooklyn. The last one said he should call her at her mother's. She wouldn't be home to greet him.

Of course. Like the time she had to stay in the city for some stupid party – or to help with the opening of her friend's bakery. Those four women ran his wife's life and she was the doormat who dropped everything to be with them. What was so special about New York? He'd been there and wasn't impressed. Pittsburgh had restaurants and sports teams, and it was a helluva lot easier to park. Besides you could see all that New York stuff on television – and not have to pay outrageous prices for the privilege.

Well, she could stay with those bitches for all he cared. He'd taken enough abuse. He'd miss Kate more than he'd miss her. Rachel had made it clear from day one he was only the step-dad. *Only the step-dad!* Those she-devils probably told her to say that. *Might as well let the child know right away instead of breaking it to her later.* He could almost hear them advising her and it chapped his butt. He should have been tipped off when she didn't change her name to his, but he gave in despite his own misgivings and his dad's raised eyebrows.

When he first met The Bitches he had mistakenly tried to win their approval and that had backfired miserably, so now he sometimes laid it on thick, just to show he didn't give a rat's ass what they thought of him. To them he was Mr. Milquetoast. Not a fancy book editor or TV producer. Not some foreigner with a woman's job who probably couldn't cut the mustard in his own damn country.

The most generous of The Bitches suggested Bob and Rachel had a deep spiritual connection, – or failing that – an amazing sex life. "Packing a sea monster" as he'd overheard Tina so delicately put it.

Bob wasn't bad-looking, tall, prematurely gray, with blue eyes and a body slim from bicycling to work. But the minute he started talking he lost points. It was uncanny – they'd all had the same reaction, as if his thin veneer of normalcy cracked and they could see the bitter, slightly scary man behind it. Nonc of them had ever understood why he and Rachel had married.

It might have been daycare. Kate was born with a brachial praxus injury and had required numerous surgeries before she was able to leave the hospital. Between the medical bills, student loans, home care and the cost of getting her veterinary practice up and running, Rachel had some rocky years during and after college. Before she and Kate moved into a group house shared by five other people including a couple who also had a small child and by good old, reliable, frequently home to watch the kiddies Tomato Bob.

Bob went to his cubicle every day and spent eight hours looking at a dizzying array of printouts. The ones with the longest green bars went into one pile and the longest red bars went into another. Mind-numbing.

He compensated with macho man activities like mountain biking and whitewater rafting, but did that carry any weight with his wife and her four bitchy friends? It did not. He knew what they called him, but he had his own words for them – not that he ever spoke them out loud. Bitch was the least of them. But that was okay. He'd soon be seeing less of them.

Brian Didrikson actively hated the airport shuttle bus. To him, it was filled with entry-level drones, schleppers, and people on packaged tours. Successful men had black cars pick them up. Drivers holding signs or nowadays iPads facing out, showing their passengers' last names in bold type. They swept by him as he trudged to the bus stand. The first time he'd had to take the shuttle it felt like a diminishment, one more step on the road to anonymity. One more confirmation that he was a failure. Did Ken Burns take the shuttle bus? Not a chance. He probably had Peter Coyote or some other narrator carry his bags for him on the way to the stretch limo.

Ken Burns had been Brian Didrikson's bête noire ever since that documentary about Coney Island. They'd met once – an impersonal group meeting at the public television station where Brian got his start. It was the kind of brief encounter the more famous person had thousands of and would have been hard pressed to recall, but the less famous one remembered his entire life and resurrected when trying to convince himself that he is, or once was, a comer. It was also the occasion of a chance remark by Brian about the movie *The Untouchables* that later convinced him he'd given Burns the idea for his series on Prohibition. He didn't. But Brian continued to nurse the belief.

In Brian's view Burns had hijacked all the best non-controversial, easy-to-love American subjects – baseball, the Civil War, jazz, national parks. What was next – the definitive eighteen-part series on apple pie? Classic Coke? No. It would surely be Brian's lifelong passion. He was terrified that one day soon Ken Burns would turn his attention to comic books and Brian's career would be snuffed out even before it started.

Only Abby Daniels had appreciated his vision. She didn't dismiss comics as puerile cartoons normal men left behind once they matured, or as that smart-mouthed Tina had put it, the young man's introduction to porn. Abby appreciated them as graphic novels, not as an excuse to look at scantily clad Amazonian women.

At least that was what she'd said when he picked her up at the train station last summer and she'd let him take the long way home.

CHAPTER 32

Abby's apartment building stood on a recently gentrified block in the East Village. Block by block the streets changed and you could generally tell who the inhabitants were by the tree gardens, window boxes and lack of graffiti. Or by the towering stacks of garbage and scurrying rodents. In the 1980s Abby's building had three times as many apartments, but over the last two or three decades apartments were combined and restored to the way they'd been in earlier days – spacious and light-filled even as they rubbed shoulders with their down-at-heel neighbors.

Two police cars blocked her street. The building's lobby was crowded with residents and onlookers whom uniformed cops vetted before letting them enter. One of them stopped Jane.

"Do you live here, miss?"

"No, I'm visiting a friend," Jane said.

"Call her. She'll understand why you're late," the cop said.

"I don't even know that she's here. The building manager called her father and he asked me to check on her. He's worried because he hasn't heard from her."

The two cops exchanged looks. "What's the apartment number?"

"3505."

"Do you have keys?"

"I have the code for the lock. What's this about?"

By that time, Vincenzo had parked the van and joined Jane in the lobby. The two cops waved them through to the elevator and radioed that someone was coming up who could get them in the apartment. One of the cops rode along with them.

"What's going on?" Jane said. "You're making me nervous." The cop said nothing.

"There's no need to be so mysterious," Vincenzo said. "You're frightening my wife." He put his arm around her protectively.

"A neighbor called. There seems to be a troubling smell coming from your friend's apartment."

"What kind of smell?"

The elevator stopped. There were three apartments on Abby's floor; her front door was across from one and at the opposite end of the hall from another. The hallway was packed with police, EMTs and building employees. A janitor was on his knees, trying to remove the door and Jane knew why. The entire floor reeked. It wasn't like anything she'd ever smelled before.

The crowd parted for her. Nervous as she was, she fumbled with the keypad, but finally entered the code and the police moved her aside to enter. Just as well. The stench was overpowering.

Jane and Vincenzo waited in the hallway. Within minutes, one of the cops returned, one hand over his nose and the other gloved hand holding the source of the smell. The remains of an exploded container of crabmeat.

"Your friend should have known this stuff has to go in the fridge," the cop said. "Hot as it's been – we're talking spontaneous combustion. Her kitchen looks like that scene from *The Exorcist*. Only it ain't pea-soup."

"She went away for the weekend," Jane said, "and hasn't returned yet."

"She's gonna have a helluva surprise when she gets back," the cop said.

Jane thanked the police and Charlie, the building manager, who was anxious to get off the floor and glad that Jane's presence meant he didn't have to clean up the mess. Jane and Vincenzo closed the door behind them.

"Could this get any weirder?" she asked. "It smells like someone died in here. A month ago. Do we clean first or look for clues?"

"You can look for clues," Vincenzo said. "I'm going to open some windows. And prevent you from even going into that kitchen."

Jane and Vincenzo tiptoed around the apartment, calling her name every once in a while even though it was clear she would have responded if she was there and not dead or passed out from the smell. Nothing seemed amiss in the living room, or bathroom. Then they entered her bedroom.

On Abby's bed sat a black quilted wheelie with a pull-out handle. It bore the repeated initials of a person or company Jane didn't recognize. The handle was scratched and it looked like a luggage tag might have been yanked off but a discreet leather flap on the back held the owner's business card – Abby Daniels.

"I should call Mac. I may condense the exploding crabmeat story, but he'll feel better knowing that she's not here, lying on the floor, overcome by gas."

"Will you tell him her suitcase is still here but she's not? Won't that make him more nervous?"

"She's got more luggage than a film star from the forties. One of her clients keeps giving her sets. She even gave me a couple of pieces."

"Cara, this one is packed and on her bed."

"I owe him a call."

The conversation with Mac Daniels was brief. Jane said the offending smell was the result of some spoiled food. She said nothing about the fruit basket, the note, spontaneous combustion, exploding crabmeat or the fear that there was a dead body in his daughter's apartment. And she didn't mention the packed suitcase, sitting on the bed waiting for someone to take a trip. Jane's voice was upbeat and so was Mac's. But the question that was left unasked was *Where the hell is Abby?*

"I'm sorry to have spoiled your evening, Jane. I'll explain to Abby that I asked you to go there. She'll understand. Will we see you and Vincenzo for Thanksgiving?"

It was their extended family get-together, a tradition that started the first November Jane's father was gone.

"Of course. We wouldn't miss it."

"Let's get out of here," Jane said, after hanging up. "Mission accomplished."

"You can tell a lot about a woman from what's in her fridge," Vincenzo said. "Under her bathroom sink, in her handbag. My father taught me that."

"Very profound. My handbag has my car keys in it, let's get going." Vincenzo stood by the bed.

"The same could be said for the way she packs a suitcase."

"Is there no end to the violations we are ready to commit in the name of concern? Mac Daniels didn't ask me to go through his daughter's personal belongings," Jane whispered.

"Don't you share a room at the Cape house?"

"What does that have to do with anything?"

"Wouldn't you have seen what was in her suitcase anyway?"

"That's pure sophistry."

Vincenzo looked puzzled. She didn't know how to explain the word in Italian. "It's a false argument. A tricky way to make your point."

"I'm not trying to be tricky, Cara. You're the one who agreed to this *mission.*"

It was true. Heaven knows, she was happier getting her feet – and everything else – rubbed instead of standing in an apartment where the kitchen walls were covered with green, wasabi-like slime.

"All right. In for a penny," she said. "Close the bedroom door, though. My eyes are starting to tear."

The bag was methodically packed. Tops were folded neatly in one stack and bottoms – shorts, yoga pants and white jeans – in another. Two pairs of shoes and two pairs of sandals were encased in separate Bendel's shoe bags. Underwear, swimsuits, bras, a matching striped laundry bag held a turquoise lace teddy and thigh-high stockings.

"I feel like a pervert," Jane said.

"Do you *all* pack like this for The Weekend?"

"Absolutely. We dance around in our sexy nighties and then invite the Latvian bartenders over."

"'Scusi?"

"Never mind. I'll explain it some other time. Check the last two smaller bags."

Her toiletries, in a third Bendel's pouch, would baffle many men, but Jane recognized they were not what most of the women brought to Wellfleet. True, sometimes one of them brought her latest must-have miracle goo as a new product alert, and once Tina had insisted on tinting everyone's eyelashes, but this paintbox could have belonged to a runway model or Vegas showgirl. Bottles and tubes which smoothed, primed, concealed, highlighted, brightened and smoked. No wonder Abby always looked so polished. Jane made a mental note of some of the product names.

The last bag was a black satin pillowcase. Jane peeked inside. "Uh-oh. Jackpot." She fished out a leather and chain contraption whose use wasn't immediately clear, but whose still-attached tag from an online retailer called The Sub Shop explained a lot.

"Were you girls planning to go horseback riding?" Vincenzo's tone was quizzical.

Jane searched for the words in Italian, but stopped struggling when a slow smile crept over Vincenzo's face. "Are you forgetting we Italians elected a porn star to parliament? We have this stuff in Italy too. In fact, I believe Leonardo may have invented the first sex toys."

She smiled in spite of herself. So who was the adventurous man Abby planned to meet before she abruptly changed her mind – or had her mind been changed for her?

CHAPTER 33

At the end of Abby's hallway a young woman laden with two canvas bags, a massive handbag, and a white plastic bag from John's Pizzeria, struggled with her keys. She was surprised to see Jane and Vincenzo coming out of Abby's apartment.

She sniffed the air and gave them a cautious smile. "Can I help you?"

"We're friends of Abby."

"I'm pretty sure she's away. What's that smell? Did something happen here."

"There was a kitchen mishap, but everything's okay now."

"Doesn't smell okay." The woman stared at Jane as if trying to place her. She put her bags down on the hallway floor. "You're one of the Bitches, aren't you?" The wariness left her face. "Abby has some neat pictures of you. There's a great one of all of you on the Cape."

Jane knew the picture the woman meant. They each had a copy, in a silver frame, Abby's Christmas present two years ago. The women sat in a row along one of the fences on the dune, leading down to the beach, their facial expressions capturing each of their personalities. A stranger walking his dog had snapped it for them.

"Isn't this the time you're usually there?"

"Yes. This past weekend actually. I'm curious," Jane said, "when did you last see Abby?"

The woman gave it some thought. "I guess it was last Wednesday night. We ordered Thai. I usually get home from work late – around this time. So does she. Some restaurants have a dollar minimum on deliveries so every once in a while we ordered takeout together and split the food. She mentioned an upcoming trip. Didn't she go?"

Jane shook her head.

"Now that I think of it" the woman said, "something strange happened that night. I was planning to order in and knocked on her door to see if she was interested. She was and she came over to wait. We were going to divvy up the food and then she said she was going back to her apartment to finish packing."

"What happened?"

"After the order arrived, we heard noise in the hallway. I thought it was the delivery man shoving menus under the other doors. I was about to go out to read him the riot act but Abby stopped me. She looked through the peephole. She had a peculiar look on her face and told me not to bother."

"Did she say who it was?" Jane asked.

"No. But she wound up eating here. I was glad for the company – she'd never done that before. She checked the peephole again before she left. As if the guy might still be there."

"Did you see what the man looked like?"

"No. She pulled me away from the door. She said she'd had the crazy feeling all day that someone had been watching her." The neighbor gave a short laugh that was more like a snort. "It'd be a miracle if guys weren't watching her. I should have so many guys beating down my door."

Jane thought it unlikely if the poor girl stayed at the office until nine every night and ate takeout alone in front of the television. But then, it was a surprise to learn that Abby did that on occasion. The golden girl who the other Bitches assumed was out partying every night. They thanked the neighbor and started toward the elevator, then Jane stopped and turned around.

"So many guys?"

There'd been a different guy the night before. And that one Abby had let in.

CHAPTER 34

"Mrs. Didrikson? Nina Mazzo. I'm wondering if I can stop by this afternoon. I'd like to bring you up to speed."

"So soon?"

Clare had been quick to whip out her checkbook to pay the woman's fee but after twenty-fours how much could she have learned?

"Perhaps we should wait until my friends are back in the area." Now that there was news she wanted the safety net of their company before she heard anything from Mazzo.

"Are you expecting them?"

"No."

"Then, at the risk of bringing up an indelicate subject, you did hire me for only two days. I thought you'd want to know what we've learned so far."

"Were you able to find out much?" she asked.

"A bit. But it's best discussed in person. Shall I come to you or would you prefer to come here?"

Clare opted for the office. Did she really want to hear bad news in her home? She remembered Tina's mother needing to paint and refurnish the room where Tina's aunt had passed away after a long illness. Tina had rolled her eyes but even as a young girl Clare understood the impulse to erase all traces of a painful memory. It had been easy enough for the three Ruggiero brothers to move the furniture and for Tina's father to paint the dull green room a sunny yellow, but if Nina Mazzo's news was bad Clare would be on her own. She could get rid of a dress or an outfit but she didn't know how she'd get rid of the chair, the sofa, *the walls*, if she sat in her own cozy living room and discovered that one or both of the most important relationships in her life – her husband and the Bitches – was crumbling.

She had a doctor's appointment that afternoon so she told Mazzo she'd stop by at five p.m.. Then she searched her closet for an outfit that she wouldn't mind trashing.

It was scary how much private information was available if one knew where to look. Forget the internet. Simply by asking – neighbors, colleagues, mailmen – one could assemble a pretty accurate picture of someone's activities. And secrets.

In addition to herself, Nina Mazzo had a small staff. A computer wizard who never left the office and ate at his desk three times a day and a couple who could, when the situation called for it, pass themselves off convincingly as newlyweds, undercover cops, social workers, delivery people, house hunters, wedding planners, you name it. Their value lay, chiefly, in their chameleon-like ability to fade into the background. Nina taught them everything they knew, but she couldn't teach them how to be young, fresh-faced and non-threatening. Those were skills they brought to the table.

Mazzo's office was in disarray. She had her sleeves

rolled up, rearranging office equipment when Clare arrived. An empty carton and Styrofoam stuffing lay scattered and a sleek, small copy machine sat where a creaky behemoth had been the day before.

"Ms. Didrikson, good to see you again. Please have a seat." With bracelets jangling she pointed to a chair.

Would she have said that if the news was bad? Clare instantly replayed Nina Mazzo's greeting, looking for hidden meanings.

"Busy today. Business always picks up this time of year. Who's to say? Girls in summer dresses? Husbands on their own while wives are down the shore? It happens."

That didn't sound promising. What was she saying? Clare's husband was one of many legions of philanderers? Was that supposed to make her feel better?

"My operatives have learned a number of things."

"Your husband had lunch with Abby Daniels last Tuesday at a French bistro on the east side of Manhattan. Café Joul. The maitre d' remembers them having a slight disagreement. At least your husband seemed upset."

Not everyone who goes to a French bistro in the afternoon is having an affair but, Clare hoped the maitre d' didn't also remember that they'd ordered oysters and champagne and played footsie under the table. When was the last time Clare and Brian had gone to a bistro in the afternoon?

"It was a business discussion. Brian told me all about it." Why was Clare lying? Hadn't she paid Mazzo to find out the truth?

"Your husband's credit card bills which you gave us authorization to look into show that on the fourteenth of June – a date you mentioned when we last met – your husband made a number of purchases from the Fairway market, from a caterer and a liquor store."

"We had a party."

Mazzo held up her hand to stop Clare from speaking. "There were two other purchases. About one hundred and seventy-five dollars at the White Horse Inn and Tavern and ninety-seven at a Victoria's Secret. Both in Winston Heights. Any idea what these purchases might have been?"

Clare shook her head in disbelief. She hadn't said anything but she'd noticed how long it took Brian and Abby to get home from the train station. She'd casually suggested the date to Mazzo as a place to start and the detective had picked up on it quickly. Had they stopped for a drink – or something more? She wouldn't miss the red jacket, which had never been flattering, but she was sorry she'd worn the black slacks. She always liked them.

"The easy part was all the flight reservations last week. If they'd driven someplace they'd have been harder to track. Your husband did fly into Heathrow. He's returning today, by the way. Tina Ruggiero's husband David is in Italy, teaching. He made and then received a phone call from Abby Daniels last Wednesday but he's on his own at the villa where the workshop is being given. He's got eight students. All male." She also knew about Vincenzo Palmieri flying to and from San Francisco.

"Palmieri seems to have had no recent contact with your missing friend but a Marco Palmieri has. Are they related?"

"Brothers," Clare said. "Omigod, was that it? One of your men? Vincenzo's brother?"

Clare was relieved for all of her friends – even if she didn't know what Brian's curious credit card charges meant. Hell, if he had decided to get drunk and wear women's underwear she'd deal with it, but at least he hadn't run off with one of her best friends. Not that she was worried.

"The interesting thing is the lady herself. Abby Daniels had a first-class ticket, New York to Miami. But she didn't show up. She doesn't seem to have flown anywhere. Oh – and your friend, Mrs. Price? Despite what she may think, her husband was not in Canyonlands National Park last week, communing with nature."

CHAPTER 35

Jane didn't want to engage in any long-winded telephone conversations about Mac's call and her visit to Abby's apartment so she texted Rachel and suggested that whoever was in Brooklyn on Tuesday night meet at an Italian restaurant near the bakery.

She made a dinner reservation for four at Minetta's, an old-school Italian place within walking distance of Sweet Dreams. She arranged to meet the others there as she was never sure exactly when she'd get out of the bakery. Some last minute task or emergency always seemed to occur and despite the surprising renewed interest of Glenn Buonofiglio all responsibilities fell squarely on Jane's shoulders.

On weekends Minetta's sported a lively bar scene. Jane and Vincenzo had several times made the mistake of going on a Thursday or Friday when the office workers (she always thought they were office workers for some reason) were cutting loose – drinking too much and talking too loud to convince themselves they were having a good time. The guys in gray suits with one hand in their pocket and the other clutching a cold beer. The women at the bar, eyeing the crop of men and wondering if any of them was worth the sacrifice of a night of Haagen-Dazs and streaming Netflix.

During the week, the clientele consisted of couples and families and it wasn't hard to be seated, even at the last minute since Jane and Vincenzo were locals who sometimes crawled in just as the kitchen was closing.

Tina and Rachel arrived early and tossed the car keys to a disinterested valet. A big-haired, big-breasted hostess seemed to recognize Jane's name, and the women waited while she officiously searched her clipboard. The name badge on her bountiful chest read Althea, and she trailed one long bejeweled nail down the page looking for the name Monaghan. She lingered over names that weren't even close. Tina got antsy. "It's Jane Monaghan. I think she comes here a lot."

Althea flapped her window-shade lashes but said nothing. She put her hand to her Bluetooth, held up one claw-like finger and turned away to take the call.

"Is Big Brother telling her where to seat us? There are tables everywhere," Tina said. "Althea . . . I wonder what she calls the other fake boob." It was less of a whisper than she thought, and with a strained smile the hostess gave her a look that Tina knew well. At dozens of Ruggiero family gatherings relatives sat in finished basements after marathon meals – mostly talking about people they didn't like. *Malocchio.* The evil eye. Tina had never been on the receiving end of one and – never discount the lessons of youth – it sent a chill through her. The hostess finished her call and told the women politely but firmly they couldn't be seated until their entire party arrived.

"Are you kidding?" Tina pointed to the empty tables.

"You're welcome to have a drink at the bar while you wait," Althea said, ignoring Tina's comment. The woman was enjoying her tiny bit of power. She had them pegged as city girls who thought they were slumming at Minetta's. They'd order trendy cocktails that Tony the bartender wouldn't know how to make and when they eventually ordered food ask about half-portions and low-fat substitutions. Then they would barely touch their meal or throw it up in the ladies room before they left the restaurant. She knew their type and disliked them on sight. And she knew a little something about these women in particular.

Short of commandeering a table, for which they'd likely be ejected, they had no recourse but to do as Mistress Althea decreed. Tina could feel the woman's eyes burning holes in her back as she and Rachel walked to a dimly lit alcove whose centerpiece was an enormous gilt-framed mirror. They climbed onto bar stools and Tina kept up a non-stop stream of snide remarks about the hostess that were juvenile and pointless but made her feel better.

"You know," Rachel said, "I think *you* were the one that people first called Bitch. The rest of us are amateurs compared to you."

"C'mon. *She* is being a bitch. She wants us to run up a drinks tab, that's all. She's probably in league with the bartender. Or Uncle Guido owns the place and she gets a bonus for every sucker she sends to the bar before dinner."

"If anyone other than an Italian said that, you'd think it offensive."

"But I am Italian so I can say it."

"Fine," Rachel said. "Let's play right into Uncle Guido's hands and get some wine."

A white-haired bartender appeared with a divided bowl of mixed nuts and potato chips so greasy they looked like they'd been drizzled with olive oil. The man was ancient, with leathery skin and a courtly manner honed a few generations past. "What are we having, signorinas?"

Tina felt better. She turned to Rachel. "What was that wine Abby turned us on to the last time we ate Italian? Two words, northern Italian, white wine." The bartender waited. Rachel looked at her blankly. Wild guess, anything other than Chianti in a raffia-clad bottle would have been considered fancy schmancy in Minetta's. Rachel nibbled on a chip. "Now I know why Monaghan likes this place. These are amazing."

"Tocai Friulano, that's it!" Tina said, slapping the bar. "We'll have a bottle of that." The bartender reacted as if they'd asked for mead or nectar from the gods. They settled for a bottle of house red.

"We're going to drink an entire bottle of wine while we wait for Jane and Clare?"

"Depends how late they are and how long that hostess continues to give me the stink-eye." Tina sucked down the first glass and Rachel kept pace. When round two was poured, Tina sarcastically raised her glass in the direction of the hostess who caught it out of the corner of her eye. The woman's smile had f.u. written all over it.

"I can't see why Jane chose this place," Tina said. "Apart from the chips, which taste better than they look, it's a little tired to me. They probably have spaghetti and meatballs on the menu."

"Don't knock spaghetti and meatballs. It's Kate's favorite dinner."

"She's a child."

"People always remember the places where they have a good time. Maybe she and Vincenzo had their first date here. Bob and I went to an IHOP. That could have been fun, but in retrospect I think it was a bad sign. Where did you go on yours and David's?"

They talked about first dates, first loves and something they called The Ninety Day Rule. It was the reason she'd never told the others about Kate's father that summer, ages ago. As young girls the group had an unwritten rule that you weren't really "seeing" someone until ninety days had passed.

No one remembered who'd come up with the formula but it did make some bizarre sense. Whatever time of year you had your first date The Ninety Day Rule was bound to include some holiday or long weekend, and for The Bitches that was the litmus test – a watershed moment in a relationship. Do you spend the holiday together? Go to the family picnic? See the tree at Rockefeller Center? Or go to the Feast of San Gennaro in Little Italy and lick powdered sugar from zeppoles off each other's lips? If you didn't the guy was just a footnote. A blip on the screen.

"You're making a nice dent in that bowl of chips," Tina said.

"I'm giving myself a base. For the wine."

The bottle was dwindling and still the others hadn't arrived. Tina checked her phone and found an earlier voicemail from Clare. "Rats. Clare had a doctor's appointment and it went late."

"Is she all right?"

"It's a message, Rachel. I can't ask it a question and expect an answer."

"Nothing from Jane?"

Tina shook her head. "We've only been here ten minutes, it just feels longer because we were early – and because the ambience is so delightful. She looked up from her phone just as two other women clambered onto the stools near them, closer than she would have chosen, given the rest of the bar was empty.

They were over-tanned, over-jeweled, overly friendly and made no secret of openly checking out Tina and Rachel. The less whorish of the two leaned over and let the bartender give her a peck on the cheek and a peek at her cleavage.

"Uncle Tony, can we get us a coupla proseccos here?"

"Sure, doll."

She slid back onto her seat, rearranging her voluminous bag and jangly plush-adorned key ring on the bar before turning to Rachel and Tina. "He's not really my uncle," she said. The powerful scent of spearmint filled the air between her and Rachel and the woman's hard but pretty face contorted with the piston-like motion of gum-cracking.

Confused, Rachel simply nodded and took another sip of wine. Was there a more appropriate response? *Who cares? Why are you telling us? Didn't your mother ever warn you about talking to strangers? Cavities? Super-tight pants causing vaginal infections?*

Uncle Tony wiped the counter before placing two flutes in front of the newcomers. "Here you go, Marie Angela. You girls on your own tonight? What's wrong with the men in this neighborhood?"

"Must be something in the air, Uncle T. Looks like it's ladies night at Minetta's. Personally, I'd rather go out with my girlfriends than go out with the wrong man. Girl could get herself into trouble doing that. What do you girls think?"

Marie Angela stared down Tina with the casual aggression of a schoolyard bully, albeit one in sprayed-on floral capris, dangerously high heels and a white studded jacket so small it could have been purchased in the children's department.

What a weird freaking place! Tina thought. *Jane never gets to choose the restaurant again.* Tina had been craving Chinese food anyway and instead found herself trapped in a Fellini movie. Or worse – Scorsese, where the women carried weapons.

"I wouldn't know," Tina said. She wiggled her left hand to show the simple Cartier band on her ring finger. "I'm married. Happily married. To a man. Not looking for love right now so I haven't had to worry about going out with the wrong person for a while."

Marie Angela turned her gaze on Rachel. "What about you, honey?"

"Me, too. Married. Got a kid, too. She keeps me home most nights. That and my charity work."

"For real?"

Rachel would lie through her teeth and claim to be rolling bandages for the war effort if it kept away the tough-talking girl who was now furiously hammering one stiletto heel on the floor. She made a heart-crossing motion with her index finger. "Scout's honor," she said.

"Who's Scout?"

"It's not a specific person – it's . . ."

"She means – for real," Tina said.

The menacing expression disappeared. The heel-tapping stopped. There was a break in the gum-cracking. She stared at the two of them again, as if re-evaluating. "Maybe I made a mistake."

Without the brass and bluster of five minutes earlier the girl looked ten years younger, like a runaway or a child playing dress-up with her mother's clothes and makeup. She flashed an awkward, apologetic smile, then she and her friend gathered their things, took their drinks and slunk down to the far end of the bar.

"No need to crowd you," she called. The hostess joined them and after a brief, but animated discussion the newcomers were seated in the dining room.

"I'm confused," Rachel whispered. "Did those women just try to pick us up?"

"Either that or they are a couple of pros who thought we were poaching on their territory. I have no idea what that was about – but here comes Jane. And if that witch at the desk doesn't seat us right now, we're leaving. But not before I fling a glass of this pissy wine in her face."

CHAPTER 36

"I'm sorry I'm late," Jane said. "All of a sudden my silent partner Glenn is making noise. This is a man who thinks cupcakes and cookies are synonyms for women and out of nowhere he's interested in the bakery business." She shook her head and half-perched onto the stool recently vacated by the gum-cracking Marie Angela. "He's been acting strangely for the last few days.

"He'd fit right in here," Tina said.

"He would. The first time I came here was with Glenn. When we became business partners. It was our celebratory dinner. They treated him like royalty."

"Do you come here a lot?"

"Not with him. That was the first and last time. With Vincenzo – maybe once a week. Why? Did the hostess give you a hard time because she knew you weren't me?"

"Was that the reason? I got the impression she gave every woman between the ages of fourteen and sixty a hard time. And her two friends approached us like a pair of hookers protecting their turf. "They're over there." She motioned to the hostess and the two women from the bar who were by then locked in conversation at one of the tables. "Look at that hair. They look like backup singers from the sixties. I'm thinking one entire can of hairspray per head."

"The blond? That's not the usual hostess. Maybe the one I know is out sick. C'mon. Take what's left of that bottle and let's get a table."

"I don't know why I'm taking it, it's terrible. Oh, yeah. I do." She topped off her glass.

"What about Clare?" Rachel asked. "The hostess didn't want to seat us because our party wasn't complete."

"We'll say she's on her way. No biggie."

They followed Jane to the hostess station where big-haired, big-boobed Althea – Tina had started to imagine that was actually on the woman's birth certificate – took her sweet time acknowledging them. But Jane knew the drill and waited patiently until the hostess said good evening to Rachel and Tina, as if the two of them hadn't already been there for half an hour.

Then came that lethal index finger again. Tapping on the clipboard like a dying woodpecker. "We had you down for four," she said. It was a reproach. She was unduly put out by it as if one diner more or less made a huge difference to her seating plan.

"One of us had to cancel for dinner," Jane said. "She may join us later for dessert. I hope that's okay."

"I see. No problem, Ms. Monaghan." She made a note on her clipboard and plucked three menus from a stack on her podium. "Right this way."

Rachel, Tina and Jane followed her to a table close to where Marie Angela and her friend were sitting.

Jane started to pull out a chair but Tina put a hand on her forearm. "This won't do," she said to Althea. "My friend has a bad back. Could we have one of those three empty booths on the other side of the room." There was no way the hostess could refuse, the place was hardly full.

"Of course." They snaked their way through the empty dining room, Althea irritated, Tina enjoying her minor triumph.

When the hostess left Jane could barely hide her amusement. "What was that about? Please tell me you're not engaged in some kind of pissing contest at one of my local haunts."

"That's one contest I'd concede – because I'm convinced that chick has a penis," she said. "It's nothing. In fact, she and her two overdressed friends are all going to be in the next book. I'm soaking up so much local color here I may have to recognize this place in the acknowledgments."

After Althea seated them, she stopped to speak with Marie Angela again. The hostess' broad back faced Jane and her friends, blocking their view of the two floozies until slowly Marie Angela leaned around Althea, her towering hairdo visible first. Like a periscope. Then her face, pale with heavy black eye makeup. She stared at Jane and the others.

"Have I missed something?" Jane said.

"That woman tried to pick us up," Rachel said, starting to feel the effects of the alcohol. "It's been so long. I was kind of flattered."

Jane peered over her opened menu, returning the stranger's stare, but smiled and nodded. "Nothing personal," she muttered, but I wouldn't have thought you and Tina were her type." She tried to place the woman. "I've seen her before."

"Nightmare?" Tina said.

"Could be a customer, but I doubt it. I usually have

a good memory for people who give me money. And she looks like she never eats."

"Let's order," Tina said. "What do you recommend?"

Minetta's was famous for its enormous portions and garlic bread dripping with butter and cheese so the women ordered two entrees and two appetizers for the three of them. Jane wouldn't help them with a second bottle of wine but didn't stop them from ordering one.

"I thought you didn't like it," Jane said.

"After a few it gets better."

They'd want a drink once she told them what she and Vincenzo had found at Abby's apartment. She ordered a glass of prosecco and a bottle of water.

"Flat or fizzy?" the waitress said, mechanically.

"Fizzy."

Tina snorted, recalling the fake choking incident with Abby's assistant. Jane didn't get the joke. "We've got some serious catching up to do." Once the waitress was gone, Tina told Jane about the visit to their friend's office and her call to the car service company.

"I think her assistant was hiding something. While we were there a lingerie delivery arrived. He said she was expecting to take it on the weekend with her, but unless she's been hiding her true feelings about us for the past twenty years, it was not for our trip to the Cape. And I did a little acting to get the car service info."

"What does that prove?" Jane said, when Tina shared what she'd learned.

"It's a piece of a puzzle. If she knew on Wednesday that she wasn't coming to the Cape why didn't she call someone?"

"She did send a message," Rachel said. "It's not as if she just didn't show up. It was very thoughtful. And it was a lovely basket." Rachel was getting drunk.

Jane's news about the packed suitcase was less vague.

"So she didn't *actually* go off with anyone," Rachel said. "There we go. Can we get some more of those chippy things from the bar?"

"Although she clearly intended to," Tina said. "And from the sound of what she packed they were going to have a rockin' good time. What you've described sounds suspiciously like *flingus interruptus*."

"Someone had a last-minute change of heart – but who? Abby or the guy?"

"The neighbor says Abby had a male friend over on Tuesday night."

"Lover?"

"Neighbor hinted at that. But she may have been projecting. I think there's a lot of television-watching at her end of the hallway."

"That lets David out. We spent last Tuesday night at my mother's. One of her seven-course meals that lasted all night. All the Ruggieros were in attendance. Not that I was worried. And if you went to Abby's building with Vincenzo, the neighbor would have recognized him. That's two down."

"And two to go?" Jane said. "C'mon, you're not still thinking it's one of our guys, are you?"

Only Rachel hadn't spoken. She simply poured another glass of wine for herself. No one had been counting but Tina was surprised to see half the bottle gone.

"Have you heard from Bob?" Jane asked, gently.

"Abby and Bob?" Rachel said. "Sex toys? Don't make me laugh. Bob's idea of foreplay is a trip to Home Depot."

Tina stifled a laugh with a piece of garlic bread.

"Sad, but true," Rachel said. "He thinks if he takes me

shopping on Saturday that merits a b.j." The wine was helping her share.

"Interesting exchange rate," Tina said. "What does a trip to Costco get him – a threesome?"

"He's in Utah," Rachel said. "I'm staying at Mom's until Kate gets back. She's at a basketball tournament upstate. She loves it there – she inherited the Catskills chip from me. *The mountains*. That's what we called them before we ever saw any *real* mountains. It's not exactly on the way but my Mom is going to swing by and pick her up on her way home from her casino trip."

"A long drive in a van full of biddies," Tina laughed. "With all that cheek-pinching Kate's face is gonna need to be iced down when she gets home. I want to see her before she goes back to Pennsylvania. I don't want her to forget me."

It wasn't likely. The Bitches had been more like aunts to her than Bob's crazy sister. She was in New Mexico living in a yurt, making and selling beeswax candles for a living. Their parents had been so – normal. Rachel wondered aloud how they'd raised two oddballs.

"Backlash," Tina said. "Apparently you turn out either exactly like your mother or the polar opposite. Seems there's no middle ground."

"Which are you?"

"You have to ask?" Tina poked through the bread basket looking for the darkest, crispiest pieces.

"I know Pennsylvania isn't that far," Rachel said, "but sometimes I wished I lived closer. Maybe I will one day."

She said that every time the women got together but after so many years Jane had stopped asking why they didn't just move. Isn't one form of insanity continuing to do the same thing but expecting a different result? A good friend knew when to talk and when to stay silent.

Especially on a recurring subject that never seemed any closer to resolution. The waitress brought their appetizers and they shared tiny plates of cheese and olives and cured meats.

"So where's Clare?" Jane asked.

"Late appointment. At least that's what her message said. Who knows? She said she'd try to make it."

"Anything new from Brian?"

"Beats me." The way she said it made Jane think she knew more than she was telling.

Whether or not Abby had been the catalyst, something was wrong between Clare and Brian. Relationships bounced back from any number of crises – and then one day they didn't. The habit of being together gets ruptured and you wonder how long it's been only habit, and not love.

"I know this looks bad," Jane said, "but I am not bitch enough to ring the death knell for Clare's marriage."

"None of us is *really* a bitch," Tina said. "Not compared to that hostess and her friends. We were severely misnamed," Tina said. "We were merely high-spirited when we were young. It took years for us to ascend to the full flower of Bitchdom. Like Brownies flying up to become Girl Scouts."

"Bitchdom?" Jane said. "Is that even a word? Rachel, you're the vet. Do they use that in kennels?"

"Why are you asking her, I'm the writer. I say anything's a word that you want to be a word."

"Your copy editor must love you."

Tina squeezed the last drop out of the bottle. Rachel must have been quietly drinking while Tina and Jane did most of the talking. What was left wouldn't have filled a shot glass.

"Have you decided where you'll leave your papers?" Jane asked.

"It's customary for successful authors to leave them to their school. Maybe Sacred Heart."

Tina had attended Catholic school for all of seven weeks in the first grade but the experience was seared into her memory. Luckily the diocese in the family's new neighborhood didn't believe in letting kids enroll once the school year had begun and once she started in public school her parents never sent her back.

"Seven weeks? Must have made quite an impression on you."

"Bad-tempered women with lethal rulers? You bet. Sister Mary Mike Tyson is probably still there tormenting the inmates. I'll try to be fair when I outline my abuse at their hands. Why not?" she said, with a shrug. "A fake memoir wouldn't be unprecedented. C'mon, I'm kidding. Rachel, what was that thing your mother used to say? That phrase?"

"Your friends wish you well, they just wish themselves better?"

"Not that." Tina waved the words away. "The other one." Like another mantra from their youth they all said it at once – "*Perish the thought*!"

The three women convulsed into laughter and soon were wiping their eyes, Rachel more vocal than the rest. A little louder, perhaps because her mother, Gilda, was at the heart of some of their most memorable moments. But maybe it was the booze. Rachel had graduated from tipsy to tight. The women were more animated as the after-work crowd trickled in and raised the decibel level. Tina lifted her empty glass for another toast, "Wherever Clare is, we hope she's having fun. And Abby. Well, I'm fairly sure she is."

Her words got a rise from Marie Angela. She leaned over to whisper to her friend, the one Tina had started to think of as Silent Babs.

"What is it with those two?" Tina said, laughing. "If they don't stop staring at us I'm going to get up and pop one of them. I am not afraid of two scrawny skanks."

"Maybe they recognize you from your website," Rachel said, starting to slur her words.

"You think they're two of the eight people not at this table who've actually visited my website?"

There was something comforting in their good-natured bickering. Sisterly. Something Jane forgot she missed until she experienced it again. She excused herself and went to the ladies room, taking another sidelong glance at the women who were so interested in her and her friends. In her absence a tall, beefy man had joined the hostess at her station and Jane returned just in time to see him snowplow through the crowd of waiting diners to the two floozies who had been staring at her and her friends. Seeing him out of context she realized he was quite handsome.

"Isn't that your partner?" Tina asked.

Jane nodded. "Now I know why those girls seemed familiar."

CHAPTER 37

Jane knew that he saw her. After a testy exchange with the other women Glenn Buonofiglio came over to her table.

"Ay – how's my favorite partner?"

"Glenn, this is getting to be a habit."

"What a coincidence – am I right? Is this empty chair for me or are you expecting someone else?"

"Our friend Clare may join us," Jane said. "You remember Tina and Rachel."

"Absolutely. The Bitches of Brooklyn. There's another one, right?"

He'd met them all at least a dozen times and had just the day before suggested pina coladas on the dunes with them so she was surprised he had to ask.

"Abby."

"Right. She gonna be here, too?"

"No," Rachel said. "We're not sure where she is tonight. Hot date probably. I had a hot date once."

"Eat some bread, Rachel. Maybe we should get her a coffee." Jane looked around for the waitress.

"Glenn," Tina said, leading with her chin, trying not to

point, "those girls over there. Are they friends of yours?"

"Yeah. Well, friends of a friend. A girl I know named Roseanne. Jane knows her too. Why?"

"They were incredibly weird when Rachel and I were sitting at the bar."

"They still are. They tried to pick ush up," Rachel slurred. "But I said I was married. I don't fool around. Like some people who shall remain nameless."

"I don't understand," he said.

"Good grief," Jane said. "Where's that coffee? She's starting to babble."

Glenn raised his hand and the waitress appeared in a flash.

"Rachel may be mistaken about that," Tina said. "Her powers of perception are a little fuzzy right now. Those two were going on about the dangers of dating the wrong man. How a girl could get in trouble. I don't know who they thought we were; just as they came in that witch of a hostess said something to them about us."

"Althea? She's my cousin."

"Sorry."

"That's okay. I don't like her much."

"Is she also a friend of Roseanne's," Jane asked.

"Like sisters."

"Roseanne doesn't still think there's something *romantic* going on between us, does she?"

Glenn looked sheepish. Despite the marriage proposals, he had to admit that Jane was not the one true love of his life.

"No. In fact, I've been meaning to tell you. I'm seeing someone else."

"After all you two have been to each other?" Tina said. "Ease up, Glenn, that was a joke."

"Ann Marie will be so pleased," Jane said. "Who's the

lucky girl?"

Rachel's double espresso came.

"Glennie, so how's it goin'? How you been?" the waitress said. "Roseanne was in earlier. She didn't say but I think she was looking for you. Stormed in, talked to Althea and stormed out. I could hear the tires screech as she pulled away in that crazy Benz. You got quite a harem goin' on. I wouldn't like to be around when Rosanne finds out you've got three dates tonight. Especially after that looker you were in with last week. Marie Angela is probably texting her now."

"Was she here when I was in last week?" Glenn asked.

"She's in every Tuesday night. She gets her nails done next door. Every Tuesday like clockwork. I don't know how she can text with those talons but she does."

Glenn's smile and exaggerated macho manner were gone, replaced by a look of concern. He stood up. "I should leave," he said, with a half-smile. "You girls are ruining my reputation."

CHAPTER 38

Before leaving the restaurant, Glenn stopped again at Marie Angela's table. Althea joined them. Voices were raised and at that point Tina wished they'd been seated closer. One thing they all heard, the words *The Chin*. The two tough-looking women exited without a glance in The Bitches direction.

More drunk than the others had seen her in years, Rachel half-rose in her seat and watched them walk away. "I wouldn't even *know* how to walk like that."

"It's the shoes. Sit down," Tina said. "Jane, I'm starting to feel like we're the dullest friends you have. What was that about?"

"There's this crazy girl Roseanne. My bookkeeper's granddaughter. She's a piece of work. She thinks she's engaged to Glenn and practically threatened to kneecap me if I so much as looked at Glenn. As if I would."

"Why not? He's good-looking. Has a certain teddy-bear swagger."

"I've already got the man I want."

"You're lucky," Rachel said. She nodded a little too

vigorously and then slid her hand to her mouth. Jane and Tina reflexively shoved their chairs back to get out of the line of fire, reliving high-school days when they'd taken turns holding back Rachel's hair as she prayed to the porcelain bus.

After a series of facial expressions that promised much worse she belched. Daintily.

"We're gonna have to rename her the Lightweight Bitch," Tina said. "I think this girl has reached her limit."

"I'm fine," Rachel said, this time hiccupping. "I just need – hup- some bread – hup! It's a matter of air in the windpipe. Dogs can hiccup. Did you know that?"

"Great, now we're getting vet trivia. Give her the garlic bread."

"It takes more than appetizers to soak up as much wine as she had. She should have had pasta."

"It's my fault," Tina said. "I shouldn't have ordered a whole bottle at the bar. I've been cranky since we got here. The hostess and those two harpies only made it worse."

"See? This is why your book is going to be a bestseller. Anyone else would have resorted to foul language to describe them. I tell Kate all the time there are other words to use. Like loser, jerk, half-wit . . . ." She drifted into a rambling monologue, then held her booze-filled head and ran her hands through her hair as if that would squeeze all the alcohol out.

"Bob isn't in Utah," she said. "I was going to tell you over the weekend but then Abby's note came and I was confused. Neither of us has been happy for years, but I found myself thinking – could it have been because of her?"

"As if," Tina said. Jane shot her a look that said shut the hell up. Plenty of couples reconciled on the way to divorce court and if that was the case with Bob and Rachel it would be difficult to take back ugly words from her friends that were intended to console.

In retrospect, Jane should have seen it – the excessive drinking – for Rachel, anyway – the occasional cutting remark. From Tina that was business as usual, but that wasn't Rachel. Not normally. Not without provocation.

"I don't know why I bothered to hide it. It was just the story I made up when we were planning the Cape weekend. I thought it would be easier to tell you in person. I didn't want to spoil things. After Abby's note it was easier to keep up the lie."

"So where is he?" Tina asked.

"Scottsdale. He got a job offer in Arizona. He wants us to move there."

"Arizona? There's no water there – how will he grow those damn tomatoes?"

"Xeriscaping," Rachel said. "It's his new passion. I don't know what he'll grow – pinion pines, saguaro – but whatever it is he'll do it without me. I can't keep paying for this one mistake my whole life. Isn't it better to cut bait than to continue living a lie?" She waited for confirmation from her friends that she'd made the right decision.

"You don't get extra credits in this life for being miserable," Tina said. "And it can't be good for Kate to see you unhappy."

"That's what's been so hard. I'm not *un*happy. He doesn't beat me or chase other women. He's not a gambler and he's good to Kate. I'm just not happy. I don't want to spend the rest of my life being *not happy*."

Even after all the alcohol, it was the simplest, most lucid, unemotional reason for a divorce her friends had ever heard. They sat in silence for a while.

"Statistics show half of all married couples will be

divorced eventually. That's 2.5 bitches," Tina said, going for a laugh. "We should thank you. You're improving the odds for the rest of us. And we can finally stop pretending to care about nematodes on his tomatoes." That did get the laugh.

"I'll actually miss the tomatoes more than him. What does that say?"

Rachel and Kate would move back to Brooklyn. To the big wonderful home where she grew up and all the women had shared happy memories. She'd make new ones. Gilda, nobody's fool, was overjoyed Rachel was finally leaving the man she'd never thought was good enough for her daughter. The words *you could do better* were not actually spoken but they hung in the air every time Gilda saw Bob. When she learned they were splitting up she practically begged her daughter to move in.

"I'm going to set up a veterinary practice in my father's old office. This way I'll be home more and Kate can see her grandmother every day without either of us having to cross the George Washington Bridge."

"Always good to avoid the GW," Tina said.

"Half my customers have pets. I'll put your business cards near the biscuit jar." The women huddled around Rachel. Supportive. Happy she was finally tossing Tomato Bob onto the compost heap.

"Maybe we can meet for dinner once a month," Rachel said, "like we used to in the old days."

Their first Wednesday-of-the-month dinners hadn't lasted long – not nearly as long as the memory of them had. Seldom did all five of them make it, the missing kept informed of the latest news via phone and email until one night Jane found herself all alone in an Indonesian restaurant on Atlantic Avenue because the others cancelled.

"We'll see," Jane said.

Nearby diners in the restaurant turned as they heard a large dog bark. It was Rachel's cell.

"Mom? Hic! How are you – are the girls winning?"

"Leave it to Cynthia Stebbins to ruin our outing," Gilda said. "Heart palpitations. Heart palpitations, my foot. She always has to be the center of attention. We found a doctor at the casino and even though he gave her a clean bill of health, she insisted we come home. It was acid. I know. I've seen her eat."

"That's too bad. Hic! I know you and the others were looking forward to it. Hic!"

"What was that?"

"Nothing – I have the hiccups," Rachel said.

"Bet you five dollars you can't hiccup."

Rachel was about to tell her mother that never worked when she realized she'd stopped hiccupping. Gilda had called Kate's coach to let the woman know she'd be picking the girl up a day early. Kate adored her grandmother and didn't mind the extra time with her – especially since she'd texted that her team had already lost in their division and the group had been in an extended period of mourning.

Most of the women in Gilda's van were grateful for the detour. All except Cynthia Stebbins who hunkered down in the back of the van assuming an attitude, secretly popping Tums, and – when anyone was looking – taking her own pulse as if she expected not to find one.

"Are you with your friends?," Gilda asked. "Have you told them the good news yet?" Few mothers would consider the dissolution of a marriage good news, but Gilda had been scouting for Tomato Bob's replacement ever since the day she met him.

She was calling from a rest stop on the highway. With a van full of cackling women and one small girl it wasn't easy coordinating pee breaks. If she limited their beverage consumption and didn't stop for dinner they could be back in Brooklyn in less than two hours.

"They're coming right home," Rachel said, after hanging up. "I can't look wasted."

Two double espressos and a final snarky interaction with Althea and the women left the restaurant. They waited for Rachel's car to be brought around and the cool night air helped Rachel sober up.

"I've been driving in the city most of the day," Tina said. "It's not so bad. Maybe David and I should get a car. It might be safer than the bicycle."

"How's the ankle?" Jane asked.

"Scabby, but a lot easier to walk on. I've got a dancer friend who swears by arnica. That helped. I still can't get over that lunatic in the Benz."

"Benz?"

"The one who sideswiped me," Tina said. "She probably killed someone, the way she was driving."

"What color Benz?" Jane asked.

"Pink. Can you get trashier than that?"

"I'm guessing you met the famous Roseanne."

"Get the hell out of here!"

"Yeah, let's," Jane said. "Before we say anything else. This place is crawling with cousins."

As close as they were, they swung by the bakery to pick up goodies. If Gilda wasn't letting her passengers eat she and Kate might be hungry.

No matter how precisely Jane planned her inventory there were always baked goods left over at the end of the day. A local man sometimes came in with his five kids and she'd let them choose whatever they wanted. The first time she didn't ask for any payment – after all, they'd have to be thrown out in the morning – but Shanika took the man's money and Jane realized that made the gesture more of a transaction and less like charity.

"Hey, boss. I'm glad you came back," she said. "Glenn was looking for you. And your friend Clare's husband called. Four times in the last two hours. He can't find his wife."

CHAPTER 39

Rachel showered to wash away the evidence of too much wine while Tina and Jane took turns calling Clare's home. Brian Didrikson was either screening calls or he'd gone looking for his wife. Neither woman had his cell number and messages left on Clare's got a prerecorded answer that the cell phone user was not in range.

"Who's her carrier," Tina said, hanging up, "Dixie Cup and String? Where could she be?"

They huddled together in Gilda Weiner's living room at a loss for what to do next when Gilda and her granddaughter arrived, one dressed for a day and night at a casino, the other in her basketball uniform – long baggy shorts, knee socks covering coltish legs and long brown hair pulled into a ponytail. She beamed when she saw the women.

"She looks more like you every day, Rachel. Come here, gorgeous. Give Aunt Tina a hug." The girl dropped her bags and ran into Tina's arms. They shared generic chat about the weekend and what they'd done in Wellfleet and Kate told them how much she'd scored in the previous day's game, but her team lost anyway. Seeing her unofficial aunts and being in the big house in Brooklyn took the sting out of it.

Gilda, nobody's fool, instantly saw something was wrong. The women gave her the broad strokes and played down their concerns, but Jane quietly tried Clare's number again, to no avail.

"Where the hell could she be?" Tina said, after the last call. Rachel made the earmuffs move.

"I'm sorry, Kate. I shouldn't have used that word. I'm just worried about Aunt Clare."

"For goodness sake, mom, I've heard the word *hell* before. I've heard all the good ones."

"Let's not have a recitation of all the bad words you know."

The women put on a good face for the girl. She was warming up to the idea of being closer to her grandmother and seeing more of her four honorary aunts – all of whom were cooler than Tomato Bob's weird sister who lived without electricity somewhere in the southwest and had a son named Moonrise. She perked up when she saw which room would be hers with its own fireplace and a large oak tree outside which she visualized clambering down, although Gilda would install steel bars on the window before she let the girl endanger herself.

It was obvious how relieved Rachel was, seated at the scarred oak table, her feet curled under her, cradling a chipped mug, the last of a misshapen set the girls had made one summer when they got into pottery courtesy of Demi Moore and Patrick Swayze.

"Honey, I realize there's a chance you may still get back together," Tina said, "but can I just say it out loud? Once? Bob is an . . . " she thought better of it and mouthed the word so that Kate, sitting on the other side of the room with her grandmother, wouldn't hear.

"*Mom*, did Aunt Tina say *a-hole*?"

"No, Kate. She said an . . . an . . . ignoramus." Rachel doubled over with laughter – the coffee and cold shower had only done so much to restore sobriety. "I couldn't think of any other noun that started with a vowel," she whispered.

"It's okay. It works," Tina said.

Gilda raised her mug of tea in silent salute. The older woman could sense the turn in the conversation so she enticed Kate with Sweet Dreams cookies and plans for redecorating her room. Yes, it could be purple, but perhaps a border and not the walls. The women recognized Gilda's negotiating skills from their own youthful dealings with her.

"And I know all the best things to do in Brooklyn," Gilda said. "– Prospect Park, the Brooklyn Cyclones – the mermaid parade."

She even promised the girl season tickets to the Brooklyn Nets, providing she kept her grades up and her vocabulary limited to the words listed in the family's Webster's Unabridged Dictionary. The book was in a place of honor on a bookstand to the left of her fireplace and had been for decades, but it was free of dust and looked for all the world as if Gilda had just used it. Kate approached it as if it was the Gutenberg Bible.

"I bet they don't even have *website* or *blog* in this."

"Then we'll find you an updated version. But it's not the new words you need to learn. Everyone knows tweet and facebook. It's the ones that have stood the test of time. Everyone needs a good dictionary. And one they can hold in their hands in case the power goes out. Come on." Kate started to ask why anyone would need to look something up in the event of a power outage but gave it up when she realized Gilda was joking.

"And we'll get you your own membership at The Brooklyn Museum," Gilda said, as they made their way up the stairs.

"Was that where *Night at the Museum* at shot?"

"I don't think so, but I have it on good authority Robert Redford has visited there."

"Who's that?" the girl said.

"We're instituting classic movie night," Gilda said. "And one night a week we'll watch *Murder, She Wrote*. Just to give you a proper cultural education."

"This is going to be good for both of them," Rachel said, watching them disappear up the stairs.

"And for you," Jane said.

"Do you think we should call again?" Tina said.

"I don't know. We've tried so many times. Did Clare seem all right to you two this morning?"

"You mean for someone who thinks her husband's been lying to her, may be cheating, and has blown most of their dough on comic books and action figures so they may not be able to adopt the kid she's had her heart set on getting? Under the circumstances she was remarkably calm."

"Right. Stupid question," Jane said. "If she didn't call one of us, who would she have called? Her sister?"

Tina and Rachel both shook their heads. "Her sister is totally absorbed in appliance research. She can't decide which fifteen thousand dollar refrigerator to buy."

"Yikes. I better hope the fridge in the bakery doesn't drop dead. Could she have gone to Florida to see her mother?"

"No way. Besides, she's not there. Clare said something about Las Vegas. Late in life her mother's developed a taste for Wayne Newton, hot slots and plaster statues."

"That's where our next reunion should be. Oxygen bars AND outlet shops. And cell service," Tina said.

Half an hour later the stairs creaked again and Gilda tiptoed down to join them on one of the two facing love-seats on either side of the fireplace.

"Kate's upstairs on my computer. She's Googling University of Connecticut's women's basketball and all the New York teams." She smiled at her daughter, imagining their upcoming evenings together. "I'll have to order fire-wood pretty soon."

Some might have considered moving back in with one's mother evidence of failure, but Rachel looked for-ward to it. It would be a readymade sanctuary.

"I've always loved this room, Mrs. Weiner."

"Thank you, Janie. My husband and I spent many hap-py hours in this room. A lot of it talking about you girls."

"We weren't so bad, were we?" Tina said, slipping off her shoes and getting comfortable.

"No. You were all good girls. No matter what you called yourselves. You gave us a few scares. That night you decided to watch the nighttime sky at the beach and each of you pretended you were at the others' for a sleepover. I called your mother because Rachel had forgotten her asth-ma medicine. We were frantic for nine hours."

"Mrs. Weiner, you're not still blaming me for that, are you?," Tina said. "That was totally Rachel's fault. What the heck did I know about the Perseid meteor showers?"

"I remember the year you all wanted to dress as Madonna for Halloween and the other mothers and I met to discuss whether or not it was appropriate. *Like a Virgin* Madonna was out but *Desperately Seeking Susan* Madonna was okay. Rubber bracelets and fake beauty marks. Wild ponytails. I cut up three good pairs of gloves for you girls.

My grandma Dora would have been horrified."

They laughed and reminisced about youthful exploits, each pointing a finger at the other for transgressions that were so distant none of the women remembered any of them in exactly the same way. Those had been wonderful times.

"Abby worried us a little," Gilda said.

Had she known about the business with Charles Monaghan?

"She was a good girl. I never believed she wasn't. But she was advanced for her age. Womanly. Even at fourteen. But it was inevitable. Children don't stay children forever. Have you heard from her?" she said, gently. Rachel hadn't told her mother about the note, just that Abby hadn't been with them on the Cape.

"Not yet, Mrs. Weiner," Jane said.

It was Jane's turn to call Clare. The phone rang four times before a groggy-sounding Brian answered. "Hey, Jane. No, I'm awake." Why did people hate to admit they were asleep when the phone rang? Was he sleeping or had he passed out?

"What's going on?" Jane said.

"Just a rough couple of days," he said. "Work. Jet lag."

He tucked the phone in the crook of his neck and rubbed his scalp with both hands to get the blood flowing. Rough barely covered it when sitting in the middle seat of a transatlantic flight had been the high point of your day. It had been all downhill for Brian from there with the crowded shuttle bus, his wife's frosty welcome and the unpleasant, but necessary admissions that followed. He would have told Clare everything in good time, but Abby's note – and the things Clare seemed to know about his meetings with Abby – forced him to work on her timetable instead of his own. He'd held back some, but she already knew the worst of it.

The project was going nowhere. Can you be over the hill at thirty-five? He felt like a teenage boy who just realized he'd never be a rock star or professional athlete. And Clare knew. They probably all knew what a loser he was and instead of being grouped together with Vincenzo, the stud who cooked and was good-looking and foreign and would probably get his own cable cooking show or David, the whatever-he-was who wrote op-ed pieces and went to parties, he'd be sitting at the kids' table with Tomato Bob, the other partner who was a disappointment. The second string. He worked at sounding chipper and unconcerned.

"Can you put Clare on?" he said. "I figured that phone of hers must be acting up again. I told her to get a new one. She need a lift?"

Clare had left for a doctor's appointment that afternoon and never made it home.

CHAPTER 40

"But she's missing," Brian said.

"Brian, she's not missing. We've been through this recently. She's not in a ditch. She's late. There's a perfectly logical reason for Clare not to be home right yet."

"Like what?"

Tina resurrected all the things the police in Connecticut had said about Abby and fed the lines to Jane who delivered them in a flat, not convincing manner. "She went shopping, went to a double feature, bumped into another friend. She left a message with Tina that she would try to meet us for dinner. What time was that?"

"I don't know . . . sixish?"

"Maybe she just needed time alone," Jane said.

Which of them wouldn't have welcomed a few days alone to sort through the mixed emotions of the last week? They'd been through the ringer, perhaps Clare more than any of them. Jane wanted to ask if they'd had a row. She might have if the others hadn't been there. She alone knew about Clare's affair and had more sympathy for Brian than the others who had assumed the worst – of him.

"And she wouldn't call me?" Brian said.

"You said her phone had been acting up."

"She couldn't borrow one?"

Tina thought she heard a sob in his voice. Well, he doesn't sound like he was planning to run away with another woman. Although maybe he was and at the eleventh hour he saw the light.

"Is there a place Clare might have gone for solitude?," Jane asked. "The house in Wellfleet – could she have gone back there?"

"They close it to renters after your week," he said.

"Do you have contact information for the owners?"

"Clare dealt with them. The house is owned by the parents of some woman we used to work with. I haven't kept in touch."

"Did Clare tell you much about what happened this weekend?"

"Just that Abby didn't show up and Tina nearly drowned. Was there more?" The question was self-consciously casual. Without it being said, they all knew a shit-storm must have come down when Brian got home.

After they hung up, Gilda broke out a dust-covered bottle of Amaretto and four cordial glasses. Only Tina said yes.

"Is it possible she's *with* Abby?" Gilda said. It was something that hadn't occurred to any of them. But why wouldn't they have called? Clare knew how anxious they'd been when only Abby was unaccounted for.

"I doubt it," Tina said, pouring a thimbleful of the sweet liqueur. "Didn't Clare go walkabout once?" After one sip she knew why the bottle was covered with dust. One bottle was a ten year supply. "Apart from that time in Wellfleet. Didn't she disappear for an entire day once?"

Only Gilda remembered. "You were sixteen," she said. "Her parents were beside themselves. There had been a spate of kidnappings and they thought she'd been taken."

As they pieced together their recollections there was one thing they all remembered vividly. Where she was found.

Jane looked at her watch. "It's probably closed by now."

"Not hard to sneak in, though," Tina said.

"Maybe if you're a sixteen year old girl, but a thirty-six year old woman?" Rachel said. "In heels?"

Jane was wearing Merrells, she'd come from the bakery. Tina wore short boots. Rachel looked at her mother and sighed. "Mom, do you have some, I don't know, *Naturalizers* or *Aerosoles* I can borrow?

"Check the closet outside my bedroom."

Rachel went upstairs to change.

"Do I want to know what you girls are doing?"

"Just going for a walk, Mrs. W. We can't sit here and do nothing."

In five minutes Rachel returned wearing the powder blue track suit her mother wore on Sunday mornings when she took seniors on their walks around Kings Plaza or Valley Stream Shopping Center. Jane and Tina stared at her as if they saw their own lives flashing before them. They'd all be wearing pastel track suits and somehow they'd all have the same hair. Short. Permed. Three of them brownish red, the other two snow white. And they'd be wearing tinted, over-sized eyeglasses like Sophia Loren. "Say nothing," Rachel warned, "or I'm not going."

Gilda planned to man the phone and order Chinese food from Choy's. She'd get enough for six because either they'd find Clare and bring her back or they'd be late and ravenous by the time they returned.

"Are we walking?" Jane asked.

"In this outfit?" Rachel said. "Get serious. It's not that far but it's after ten so parking shouldn't be a problem. And if she's where we think she is, she's been on her feet all day so she'll be exhausted. I'm okay to drive. The sight of myself in this outfit has turned me stone cold sober."

They piled into the car, Jane in front and Tina, snickering, in the rear, and Rachel backed out of her mother's narrow driveway, relocked the gate and headed for Flatbush Avenue and Empire Boulevard.

Tina tapped away at her phone as they drove. "Yup. March through November it closes at six. I wish we had thought of this earlier then we could have walked in like normal people."

They drove slowly past the main entrance, the tall iron gate clearly locked. There was a parking spot right in front, but there were too many streetlights and it would have been obvious to anyone in the establishments kitty-cornered across the intersection or driving by that the women were breaking in.

"Pull around to the Washington Avenue side," Tina said. "There are probably fewer lights there."

"Right," Rachel said, "that's where the crackheads go because it's nice and private."

Tina dismissed Rachel's concerns. "This area's gentrified now. David and I even looked at apartments on this block."

"Is there any place you haven't fantasized living?"

"We're just keeping our options open."

Rachel circled the block and slid into a spot not far from a streetlight. She killed the engine and sat with her hands gripping the steering wheel. "You know, this seemed like a reasonable thing to do thirty minutes ago, but I'm having second thoughts. She might not even be here."

"And if she's not," Tina said, "we'll have had a good workout and we'll be able to eat mountains of Chinese food with nary a regret." Tina had her hand on the door handle but waited for the unanimous vote. "All in?" Rachel nodded.

As the swing vote, it was up to Jane. She thought about the two beat cops who sometimes stopped at Sweet Dreams after their shift ended – coffee light with a chocolate chip scone and diet coke with a mini-bear claw when she had them. She wondered if they were still on duty and whether or not the women were in their jurisdiction. It would be embarrassing for a responsible businesswoman to be caught breaking and entering.

"We're already here," Tina said. "Can't hurt to look."

"Fine," Jane said. "Let's break into the Brooklyn Botanic Garden."

CHAPTER 41

"Do you have a flashlight in the trunk?" Jane said.

"Yes. With all of my other breaking and entering gear. Wait over there, I'll get it."

"Why? Do you have a body stashed in there?"

"Okay. Fine." Rachel popped the trunk and fished around, with the others looking over her shoulder. The trunk was neatly packed with matching, compartmentalized nylon bags.

"I've seen these things on late night television," Tina said. "They're for holding bags of groceries upright, so your grapefruits don't roll around when you make a turn, right?"

"They're for holding whatever you put in them, Tina. They fold down when they're empty so they're very useful."

"What *is* all this stuff?"

"I knew you were going to ask. That's why I didn't want you to see. They're our Go bags." Even in the fading light, she could see that Jane and Tina didn't know what she was talking about. "In the event of an emergency. We've got a water purification kit, vitamins, energy bars, powdered drinks, mylar blankets, batteries, a radio. Bob made a list."

Tina was about to make a crack when Jane silenced her with a pinch.

"Good idea," Jane said. "Anything else in there we might be able to use." Rachel poked through the bags, each item causing Tina's eyes to roll.

"In the event of an nuclear holocaust or natural disaster," she whispered, "I do not want to drink Crystal Light. I want caffeine and real Coke. I want to get drunk and have casual sex. And if there's time, get a tan. I *miss* getting a tan."

"That's what you say now. Wait until you have a kid. Then you'll want an escape strategy." She held up a bundle of rope. "How about this?"

"Bring it," Jane said. "You never know. We may have your Ashley Judd moment after all."

Tina had found a map of the Garden online on her phone and learned there was a second entrance on Washington Street. They walked about half a block and climbed a short steep set of steps not far from the back of The Brooklyn Museum. They heard something, a squeak, and stopped.

"What's that sound?" Tina whispered.

"My mother's shoes. There's nothing I can do about it so shut up. I'm already walking so gingerly I'm going to give myself a cramp."

They turned left. As expected, the entrance was locked. The surrounding gate was about seven feet high with sharp finials every six inches. And the bars were smooth, they'd be difficult to grab onto.

"Even if we could climb that," Tina said, "those points could do a lot of damage. I haven't been in Mrs. Schachter's gym class for a long time and I'm pretty sure I claimed to have my period the day we had to climb the wall."

"I think you made medical history the year we had Mrs. Schachter. Anyone bleeding that much should have been in intensive care." Jane looked around for something to stand on. She and Rachel tried dragging a bench over, then realized it was bolted to the ground.

"Where's the trust?" Tina said. It was getting darker. If they didn't get in soon it would be even harder to search all thirty-nine acres of gardens.

"I got it," she said. "We turn those garbage cans upside down, stand on them and climb over the ticket booth." The others weren't so sure. "You have a better idea? It beats getting impaled on the fence." Her friends saw the logic in that and each of them dragged a heavy wire trash container over to the ticket booth.

"Take out the trash bag and tie a knot in the top. We don't need to make a mess."

"Smart," Rachel said. "Maybe they'll show us leniency after we're arrested because we didn't litter."

Jane was the first to try it. She was the tallest and still she wasn't high enough off the ground to reach the top of the ticket booth.

"Won't work," Rachel said. "Let's go."

"Not yet," Jane said, climbing down. "We can make a pyramid with the three cans. This time I'll go last in case you two need help getting over."

They stacked the cans, two on the bottom and the third on top, in the middle.

"This is like cheerleading. I'm game." Tina clambered to the top of the highest can. "It's a little bit wobbly. Not saying I can't do it. Just need encouragement. The ankle is still a little dodgy."

"How about looping the rope around your waist and then around the iron finial on top of the booth?" Jane said.

"It's not going to bend back is it?"

"How much do you weigh? Of course not. That finial's been here for over a hundred years."

"You two do this often?" Rachel asked, as her friends double-tied the knots.

"It's a sideline," Jane said, "in case the book and the bakery don't work out. Ann-Marie's nephew is a second story man and taught me everything I know."

"I'm up." Tina clung to the top of the ticket booth. "I'm going to have to untie some of this knot to rappel down the other side but it's not that far. Then I'll throw the rope back over." She did that and upended another garbage can so her friends would have a shorter way down. "That was easier than it looked," she said. "And kind of fun. Now I'm sorry I blew off that class. *Walk that wall! Walk that wall!*"

"I'm not a Marine," Rachel muttered. "I'm a vet. I'm a mother. I can't believe I'm doing this."

When all three were inside, they did their best to move the garbage can and dangling rope out of the light so that all a passerby might see were three newly emptied cans on the other side.

"Hopefully they'll think the Doe Fund was here." Tina punched in the URL for the Brooklyn Botanic Garden's map again. "All right there are only two official entrances so let's make sure we find our way back to this one. Any idea where to start?"

"She always liked the Japanese Garden."

"Do you think they have security?"

"It's New York," Tina said, "there's always security. But this place is huge – we just have to avoid them."

"That sounds remarkably like what you said the time we got caught shoplifting. Remember how well that worked out?"

"This will be different. We won't be sneaking out with plants under our shirts."

The image on Tina's phone was small but once they got their bearings and knew where they'd landed, they walked toward the Japanese Garden. The signage was perfect.

"Wow. I'd forgotten how amazing this place is. Vincenzo and I used to come here for picnic lunches sometimes but we've gotten so busy it's been years. Probably not since they had the corpse flower exhibit in the greenhouse. It really does smell like a dead body – or . . . what you think a body must smell like."

"Can we change the subject?" Rachel said. "If I smell anything remotely funky, I'm not going to wait around to figure out whether it's a body or a plant."

They moved through the Shakespeare Garden and quickly reached their destination. Clare had volunteered at The Brooklyn Botanic Garden as a teen and had talked the others into helping plant thousands of bulbs one fall. Like Rachel she'd participated in a slew of extra-curricular activities, although with her grades she could have stayed home and played Atari games and schools still would have wanted her. The day she gave her parents such a scare she'd been discovered in the Japanese Garden well after all the other volunteers had gone home. The employee who found her said that she had just been sitting, staring at the pond.

She never said what was wrong or why she'd done it, just that she'd needed time alone and between her family, her friends and her after school commitments, it was the quietest, most peaceful place she knew. She just lost track of time.

There was something wonderful about being in the Botanic Garden at night. It was as if the women owned the place. They could pretend they were chatelaines of a great country estate and they were simply taking a turn around the garden before retiring to high tea.

But they weren't. In the distance Jane thought she saw movement so she pulled the others behind a thick viburnum until the coast was clear.

"Guard?" Rachel asked.

"Who knows? But if it's *not* a guard I want him to see us even less."

"Good point."

Not wanting to split up, they searched that section of the garden together – the tea pavilion, the bridge, the path to the stone lanterns – no Clare.

They came to the Celebrity path and followed the stones honoring notable Brooklynites from Jackie Robinson to Marisa Tomei. From Lauren Bacall to Larry King.

"Tina, when your book comes out you should get a steppingstone here. Why not..there's one for Didi Conn. You don't have to be uber-famous."

None of them could remember any other spot that held a special meaning for Clare, but having taken the trouble to break in, they thought they should make a thorough search and they circumnavigated the garden. Past the conservatory to Empire Boulevard, down the Flatbush Avenue side and all the way to the

Osborne Garden near the Eastern Parkway entrance. It had taken them close to an hour and they ended their search on one of the stone benches in the garden.

The Osborne was a formal part of the garden with a large central fountain. In the spring it was a riot of color thanks to hundreds of azaleas, rhododendrons and dogwoods. At that time of year and at that hour it had the look of a vintage black and white photograph and it wouldn't have been out of place to see a man in a top hat strolling arm in arm with a woman wearing a long dress and carrying a parasol. Or a woman in white.

"I really thought she'd be here," Tina said. "I guess we're not kids anymore. Maybe we don't know each other as well as we think we do.

"We tried," Rachel said. "Let's get out of here. There's a scallion pancake at home with my name on it. In fact, Clare is probably home having dinner with Brian right now. Not a word to my mother or Kate about this."

"Wasn't there something special about this place?" Jane said. She struggled to remember. "Yes. It's like that place in Grand Central, near The Oyster Bar where you can whisper into one corner and someone can hear you clearly all the way on the other side of the floor. I think it has something to do with the acoustics or the shape of the roof."

"There's no roof here, just the firmament, darlin'."

"They're called Whispering Benches," a voice said, from the other side of the fountain. "Don't know why it works, but it does. You've got an excellent memory, Janie."

And out of the darkness, walking toward them and carrying a small overnight bag was their friend Clare Didrikson.

CHAPTER 42

"I got to Brooklyn earlier than I expected and too early for dinner so I thought I'd visit the garden. I must have dozed off in the Rose Garden."

By the time Clare woke all the exits were locked.

"I walked the entire garden twice but either I missed the security guard or he's sleeping it off somewhere so I came to the Osborne Garden because I knew there were benches here. How do we get out of here? I can't go out the way I came."

"C'mon," Rachel said. "We take Woody Allen to Barbra Streisand, make a left at William Shakespeare, climb over the booth and then down to Washington."

"I'm not sure I know what she just said."

"Pay no attention. She's just pissed because she's wearing her mother's jogging suit and the rest of us look relatively normal. Let me get your bag. You've been schlepping it all day." Jane picked up the bag which was heavier than she expected it to be.

"What's in here? Rocks?"

"I had some errands to do. Bought some make-up. A

hundred and forty dollars worth of war paint and I know I'm going to feel like a clown or a whore the minute I put it on."

"I'd have to sell eighty-four cookies to take that in. That make-up better be good."

"Not just make-up. Protein drinks. Vitamins," Clare explained. Was it ammunition to win her husband back or an arsenal to get back in the game once he was gone? Clare didn't say.

When they arrived at the locked gate, Tina showed her the drill. She happily clambered over the top of the ticket booth and slipped down, out of view, then reappeared on the other side of the gate and tossed the rope over for Clare, who knelt on one upturned garbage can and slowly rose to her feet.

"You did this for me?" Clare said, breathing heavily.

"Of course," Jane said. "And to be a scene in Tina's next book. The last six days have been all research."

"I'm touched. Really." Clare turned, hands on hips, balanced precariously on top of one of the garbage cans.

"I like the sisterly sentiments as much as anyone, but even the laziest, least conscientious night watchman on the planet might notice a tall, blond standing on a garbage can who looks like she's about to make a speech. Can we save the *Evita* moment until later? Just get on the top and hoist yourself over."

"I can't. I'm going to be a mother."

"Good. And we all promise not to tell your child what crazy-ass stunts we pulled before the holy mantle of motherhood descended upon you. Now get your butt over that ticket booth. Gilda's ordering from Choy's and it's probably arriving right now."

Ordinarily that would have been all the incentive Clare would have needed. She hadn't had decent Chinese food since she moved to Connecticut, but she stood stock still.

"No," Clare said. "I'm going to have a baby. I'm pregnant. I don't think I should risk it."

It took a few minutes for the news to sink in. The others helped her down from the garbage can. Tina, not unhappily, flung herself over the ticket booth for a third time.

"I saw the gynecologist today," Clare said. "Not exactly making medical history but I will need plenty of bed rest. And it will be touch and go as to whether I can carry a pregnancy to full term but it's a start."

"Holy shit, that's wonderful. What does Brian think?"

"He doesn't know. After the doctor I saw Nina Mazzo. I walked around, took myself to lunch, went to a movie and then came here."

"Who's Nina Mazzo?" Jane asked.

"A private investigator. I found her on a placemat. She told me some stuff about Brian and Abby . . . "

"You girls have been busy. It doesn't matter. You have to call him. He'll be thrilled. He was worried about you."

"I would have but my phone's not working. The tracking ball is stuck. I thought it was a sign that I should hold off on telling anyone."

Tina's phone did work but they had another call to make first since climbing over the ticket booth was no longer an option. The Botanic Garden office number played a prerecorded message so the women were forced to call 911 and they waited near the Washington Avenue entrance until the police arrived with a BBG employee to let them out.

As the creative Bitch, Tina concocted an implausible story of how they'd all gotten locked in, even as her eyes guiltily strayed to the track marks and overturned garbage cans near the ticket booth. Luckily Rachel had had the presence of mind to stash the rope in Clare's bag just as the cops had arrived.

"Surprising that you waited so long to call for help," the cop said, looking at the neatly tied garbage bags. "Do you ladies have some i.d.?"

They all whipped out their driver's licenses, eager to prove they were good upstanding citizens. Jane couldn't be sure but she was convinced Rachel's powder blue track suit made the cop think this was an institutional outing gone horribly wrong.

Back at Gilda's, the women nuked and plated Chinese food that had gone cold while they gave their statements to the police. Rachel's mom led Clare to her husband's former office where she could have some privacy when she spoke to Brian. They strained their ears for sounds of joy or sorrow coming from behind the closed door. When she rejoined them in the kitchen they waited until she was ready to talk.

"He's in almost as much shock as I am. But I think he's genuinely delighted. He thought I had left him."

Some men needed a drastic wakeup call, maybe this was Brian's.

"Brian was embarrassed," she said. " He'd shanghai-ed Abby at the pool party at the beginning of the summer. He took her for drinks before they came back to the house."

Playing the high roller, Brian had ordered a bottle of champagne at a tavern in Winston Heights. Abby had always been supportive of his project, but it was in her nature to be positive. She hadn't wanted to blow him off. He asked Abby to see if her father might be interested in funding the production and she agreed to broach the subject with him.

"They met last week in New York. She told him Mac wasn't interested."

Clare's husband was running out of options. He didn't

want to spend the money to go to England to look for investors since it was such a long shot. It was a last resort. And it hadn't worked.

"The reason he pushed so hard was that he had hoped it would all be settled by the time we left for the Ukraine to pick up the baby. He didn't want me to be worried about money."

From philandering husband to doting father-to-be? From possible Jezebel to helpful friend? In six days. One day, really. Why was it so hard for people to say what they really mean? How they really feel?

"Brian suggested I spend the night here, if that's okay. He doesn't want me to have to take the subway and then the train at this hour" she said. "He'll pick me up tomorrow morning. Is that all right?"

"Of course," Rachel said. "In honor of your delicate condition you can have my room. I'll bunk with Kate."

"I'm staying too. David's still away. I told him he'd better bring me something Italian when he comes home. Preferably leather."

Rachel coughed and motioned to her mother, who'd been sitting quietly through Clare's news, but had just gotten up to set the table for the Chinese food which was once again getting cold. Tina was thinking handbag, Rachel the bondage gear Jane had found in Abby's suitcase.

"Get your mind out of the gutter!" Tina said. "A handbag or gloves. A bustier, if he happened to see one. Dibs on the loveseat." They all looked at Jane. Four of them sleeping in the Weiner home. That probably hadn't happened for twenty years.

"I need to play this one by ear. It's already late for me and I have to be at work at five a.m. tomorrow. Besides, I haven't seen much of Vincenzo lately. Remember him?" She was thinking about that foot massage and what had come after. No. One spring roll and she'd be on her way home. Whatever had happened that past weekend, four of the Bitches were fine. And the fifth? She'd show up when she showed up. Abby always landed on her feet.

"What does this do to the adoption?" she asked.

"On hold indefinitely. I emailed the agency as soon as I found out but I don't want to jinx it so I won't say anymore until another three months have passed. I can defer without cancelling. It means we might not get the same baby. But what guarantees do any of us have?"

"Ain't that the truth?"

"So, today I learned that I'm going to have a baby, I met with a private eye, treated myself to tea at the Peninsula, had a small shopping spree, had to be rescued by my friends and the police, reconciled with my husband and now that I'm eating for two I'm gorging myself on the best Chinese food in Brooklyn. What did you ladies do since I saw you last?"

Tina was about to launch into her Minetta's story when they heard a furious tapping on the Weiners' side door. Rachel and Gilda both got up.

"I'll get it, Mom, you've had a long day." Jane went with her and the others waited in the kitchen. Moments later they returned.

CHAPTER 43

"Have you eaten?"

Rachel Weiner was convinced if burglars or aliens ever entered Gilda's home she wouldn't scream or faint, she'd ask if they'd eaten.

Abby Daniels looked spectacular. Well-rested, fit and positively glowing. Glenn Buonofiglio had a black eye but was in good spirits. They were holding hands.

"And how was *your* weekend?" Tina asked. Busting to say more.

"A rocky start. My travel arrangements were courtesy of a psychopath named Roseanne and her equally deranged brother."

Jane burst out laughing. "Joey the Chin?"

"Come to think of it, he *didn't* have a chin. Do you know those lunatics?"

"Not as well as you seem to. Roseanne threatened to rearrange my face if I did what you seem to have done. *One of our men?* Glenn?"

"Who did you think? Abby said. She put a small weekend bag down on the floor and perched on a stool near the kitchen's island.

Why tell her any of them had been worried? "Tina's dentist was the bookmaker's favorite," Jane said.

"You know how Tina is always saying you have one regular and my spare? Well," Abby said, "I hate to break it to you but you need a new spare."

"No way," Tina said.

"Hey, what am I?" Glenn said. "Chopped liver?"

"Chopped liver is not bad for you," Gilda said. "In small doses.

"I called my father first. Then Jane. Vincenzo told me you were all here so Glenn and I came straight over."

"What did you mean *travel arrangements*?"

"Why didn't you tell me you were seeing Glenn?" Jane asked.

"One at a time! Ninety day rule," she shrugged. "It's only been a few weeks. I didn't think I needed to send out announcements. There have actually been a few men I've dated that you've never met."

"Is that why he's been hanging around the bakery so much?"

"Has he?"

"I stopped by first thing on Monday morning," Glenn said.

Abby grabbed Glenn's arm and pulled him close. "That's so sweet. He probably wanted to know why I didn't show up at the hotel where we'd planned to meet. He must have thought I'd changed my mind and gone to the Cape with you."

"Why did you change your mind?" Jane asked.

"I had some help."

Abby's morning had started like a lot of others. An early workout. One out-of-the-office breakfast meeting. But Abby had agreed to get an early start on the weekend so she cancelled her meetings in Connecticut and changed the destination she gave to the Black Diamond Car Service. She was all packed except for a last minute present she expected to be delivered at the office which she'd pick up after breakfast.

It was to be her first trip with her new man. No one she knew would ever have expected them to be together and she too was surprised to find herself packed and ready to fly to Miami to spend four days with Glenn Buonofiglio.

For years she'd dated the same man. Not literally, but they were all the same. Cultured, worldly, well-heeled or soon-to-be. Men who knew what was hip, fashionable or trendy. And cared. Glenn was nothing if not a departure. His construction company was doing well. And despite the whiff of illegality, he said it was totally legit. The rough edges added to his appeal. Maybe she was bored. Maybe it was the frisson of danger.

She'd been having dinner with Jane at a red checkered tablecloth Italian place near Sweet Dreams. They'd been talking about Tina's book and how the two of them might throw a party for her. Glenn strode in as if he owned the joint, bypassed the hostess station and came straight to their table. She'd felt something right away. It didn't hurt that he had a rock hard body, a tan that looked like it hadn't come from a bottle or a bed and a smile that could get you wet at thirty paces. After a brief chat with Jane and a simple nod in Abby's direction he joined his friends a few tables away but her gaze kept drifting back to him. And he'd been looking at her.

Jane hadn't noticed. From that point on Abby half-heard whatever they'd been discussing. She sat in the restaurant pretending to listen but really wondering what Jane's business partner looked like without his shirt on. What the pattern of his chest hair was like – she could tell from his rolled up shirtsleeves there would be a fair amount of it. That was a plus. She wondered what his slightly calloused hands might feel like on her bare skin.

The first package arrived at her office the next day. A bag from La Perla with a turquoise lace nightie. Stretchy, thigh-high in the front with a slit in the back, maybe a drop too small, which was just right. The man had an eye for size and style. It came with a note telling her what he would do to her while she was wearing it. Hands down, better than flowers or chocolates.

Three packages were delivered before the day her phone rang and by that time there was no way Abby was not going to find out if Glenn Buonofiglio was half as interesting as his note cards and taste in lingerie promised.

The sex had been world-class. An accordion player in Bitches slang – a man who could move his fingers and push in and out at the same time. He knew exactly what she'd respond to and what to say. He was a talker. Abby liked that. She hated a man who grunted for two minutes and then smiled at her as if something wonderful had just happened. Or worse, turned the television on to the stock channel. And Glenn found places on her body most men couldn't find with a GPS.

The packages kept coming, even after their first night together. That was nice too. It wasn't all pre-conjugal enthusiasm that evaporated once the conquest had been made. She'd had too many of those.

The latest arrival came in a plain unmarked box that was all the more exciting because he'd asked her to check a website and item number online to see if she was game. She'd said yes. For this particular item, one size fit all. It sat on the credenza in her office all day and she could hardly concentrate on the current campaign until she was able to draw the shades to her office, lock the door and open her special gift from a shop that catered to adults with special interests.

Out of bed, he was a sweetheart. Glenn Buonofiglio was a handsome gruff bear of a man, smart and sensitive, once he dropped the macho posturing that seemed obligatory in his circle. He told her he cared about family, friends, America and homemade cannoli, not necessarily in that order, and he said it with a straight face that hid a wicked sense of humor.

On paper, there were a hundred reasons they shouldn't be together. But Abby had never been one to do the safe, expected thing. If the weekend went well, they'd go public with their relationship on Monday. If not, it would become an amusing anecdote told over drinks at next year's visit to the Cape. A sidebar to a rich and varied sexual history which had included one congressman, one professional football player and one best-selling author. This weekend would be the litmus test.

That's what she'd been thinking when the car came to pick her up. It wasn't her usual driver, but the car service never guaranteed a certain car or driver so Abby didn't think much of it when the slim, greasy-haired man without a chin looked her up and down, held the door for her and then climbed into the driver's seat.

"You must have been terrified," Gilda said.

"Not right away. I wasn't paying attention. We seemed to be going in the right direction for the airport and then I guess I drifted for a while." No need to tell a seventy year old woman where her thoughts had strayed, although Gilda had had cable for years and wouldn't have been too shocked. "Some idiot called the car service pretending to be one of my employees. Can you believe it?"

Jane and Tina traded glances. "Shocking," Jane said.

"This Roseanne – or someone she knows – cancelled my car and psycho-boy picked me up instead."

"You poor girl. Did they feed you?"

"Mom, not the hot issue now."

Before Abby knew it the driver claimed there was a minor problem with the car and they needed to find a service station. He pulled the car into a body shop on MacDonald Avenue and the corrugated door rolled down behind them.

"He seemed to know the mechanic, but whatever it was took forever. He said he called the car service for another car and driver but now of course, I don't believe he did. I think he called his sister and asked her what to do with me."

"They're not really dangerous," Glenn said. "Excitable."

"Did The Chin do that?" Tina asked, pointing to Glenn's black and swollen eye. She was loving it – it would all go in the next book.

"I can take The Chin. I have thirty pounds on him. This was Roseanne. Our imaginary engagement is officially broken."

"By the time they let me out of that garage I had missed my flight to Miami."

"I had business there, that's why I left on an earlier flight. Afterward, we were gonna meet at the Eden Roc Hotel. I have a friend there who was gonna give us the best room in the house."

"A good choice," Gilda said, nodding in agreement. "They have a lovely buffet. Lou and I were there in the 70's. The brisket was wonderful."

"I couldn't reach Glenn on his cell," Abby said, "so I called the hotel to leave a message that I'd be on a later flight. You know what they told me? That he hadn't arrived but

– get this, his *wife* had."

"He's married?" Gilda asked.

"Of course not, Mrs. Weiner. But this Roseanne person seems to think they've been betrothed since infancy."

Abby started looking for another flight to Miami, but was so furious she took a cab home instead. In the cab she kept checking messages to see if Glenn had called and picked up one from a prospective client with a spa in Maryland. She dropped her suitcase at home, had a bite to eat, packed a small bag and spent the last five days getting buffed, sandblasted and oiled.

"I've been living on apple cider vinegar and maple sugar for days. How do I look?"

"Great. But your kitchen's another story. Before you left," Jane said, "did you, by any chance, treat yourself to some crabmeat salad?"

"How in the world did you know that?"

"Leave crabmeat salad out in a hot, enclosed apartment for five days and ka-boom. Spontaneous combustion. Your building manager thought there was a gas leak in your apartment. Someone thought there was a dead body. They couldn't reach you so they called Mac. He was worried and asked me to check on you. You didn't see a message about it?"

"At the risk of sounding obnoxious, I get about four hundred emails a day. The one from the super is the last I'm going to open."

"Why didn't you ask Janie about Glenn?"

"I should have. But we all have our secrets. Did you have fun on the Cape without me?"

"Oh, you know," Tina said, "same old, same old."

CHAPTER 44

One year later

"You brought her!"

Clare nodded. "Showing her the old neighborhood." She settled in, arranging the baby carrier, on a small loveseat in Kleinfeld's while Jane plowed through a rack of wedding gowns.

"No meringues," Tina said. "We're Bitches, not Barbies."

"Don't worry. I'm keeping it simple."

"Famous last words," Rachel muttered.

"And I'm not going to ask all of you to wear the same dress," Jane said. "Just find something you like that's long and navy. Everyone looks good in navy – new mothers, best-selling authors, newly single doctors and recently engaged publicists. Unless you want to wear the same dress."

After the fourth gown, a salesperson brought out a tray with five champagne flutes presumably to help them decide. And it did. They raised their glasses.

"Here's to the Bitches, all present and accounted for. Including our newest member, Xena Didrikson."

EPILOGUE

Rachel Weiner and **Tomato Bob Price** divorced. She is dating a dermatologist, the son of one of her mother's mall-walking companions. Gilda thinks she couldn't do better – and Rachel's skin looks amazing.

Tina Ruggiero's novel made the New York Times extended list thanks to the efforts of Abby Daniels. She is hard at work on book two, the story of a woman menaced and then, kidnapped by her boyfriend's psychotic ex-lover. The film rights have already been optioned.

Clare Didrikson's husband Brian had no trouble getting funding for an HBO documentary on jazz violinists Stephane Grapelli and Joe Venuti, helped in part by Louis Weiner's extensive collection of records, tapes and memorabilia. As with their baby, **Clare** co-produced.

Abby Daniels and **Glenn Buonofiglio** passed the ninety day point but they are taking it slow. They did finally get to The Eden Roc in Miami where they agreed the buffet was wonderful. They never dine at Minetta's.

Jane Monaghan and Vincenzo Palmieri were married in the Brooklyn Botanic Garden. **Kate Weiner** was a flower girl. **Charles Monaghan** was never heard from again.

The Bitches gave her away.

ACKNOWLEDGMENTS

Many thanks to my agent Deborah Schneider for her continued support and her belief in *The Bitches of Brooklyn*. Thanks to Becky Indrio and the Literary Giants Book Club who read an early version and let me temporarily join their group for one awesome night. Thanks to a wonderful editor, Chris Roerden and to 99 Designs for introducing me to Abby Giducos, who created the terrific cover for *Bitches*. And to the folks at Vook for seamlessly handling the digital conversion.

Writing the book brought back a lot of wonderful Brooklyn memories so I would be remiss if I didn't thank all the Brooklyn girls – past and present – who have helped me fill the pages of this book – Fran, Susan, Beverly, Michele, Pam, Gayle, Paula, Jane, Robyne, Kay, Elayna, Donna, Marian, Margaret, Sandy, Carma, Becky, Linda, Hope, Lois, Karen . . . if I've forgotten anyone it was (possibly) unintentional. Feel free to call me a bitch.

And as always, thanks to Bruce – who is a better catch than any of the men in this book.

If you've enjoyed this book, don't forget to check out
Rosemary's other books

Pushing Up Daisies
The Big Dirt Nap
Dead Head
Slugfest

. . . and visit her website www.rosemaryharris.com for information on new releases, appearances, newsletters, giveaways and special programs for libraries and book groups.

Chestnut Hill Books
Box 284
1127 High Ridge Road
Stamford, CT 06905

Made in the USA
Charleston, SC
24 May 2014